DAMAGE

D0452436

 *titles*

DAMAGE

Sue Mayfield

Hodder
Children's
Books

A division of Hodder Headline Limited

A Catalogue record for this book is available from
the British Library

ISBN-10: 0 340 89325 7
ISBN-13: 978 0 340 89325 5

Typeset in Palatino by Avon DataSet Ltd,
Bidford-on-Avon, Warwickshire

Printed and bound in Great Britain by
Bookmarque Ltd, Croydon, Surrey

The paper and board used in this paperback are natural
recyclable products made from wood grown in sustainable
forests. The manufacturing processes conform to the
environmental regulations of the country of origin.

Hodder Children's Books
a division of Hodder Headline Limited
338 Euston Road
London NW1 3BH

For my brother Mick and my sister Jen,
with love.

Acknowledgements

Many people have helped me in writing this book. I am indebted to Inspector Paul Gilroy of Northumbria Police whose time and expertise were invaluable in authenticating the story. I am also grateful to the staff of Ashfield Young Offenders' Institute in Bristol – especially Elaine Pope (Head of Learning and Skills), Tim Clifford (Education Manager) and Ian Tyrrell (Enrichment Co-ordinator) – for allowing me to visit and pick their brains. I'd like to thank my brother Mick, my husband Tim, my sons Frank, Jonah and George and my friend Gillian for being my sounding-boards and keeping me going. And thanks, as ever, to Emily Thomas, for painstaking editing, and to my agent Elizabeth Roy.

Although many details of the storyline resemble events in real life, all the characters and incidents described are fictional and any similarities to specific traffic accidents are coincidental. *Damage* was written between October 2004 and March 2005.

Visit Sue Mayfield's website: www.suemayfield.com

List of Characters

Matt Fry – a Sixth Former
Becci – Matt's sister
Sally – Matt's mother
David – Matt's father
Nathan – Matt's friend
Stella – Nathan's mother
Mike – Nathan's father
Jack – Nathan's younger brother
Sophie – Matt's girlfriend
Kirsty – Sophie's mother
Gary – Kirsty's 'date'
Emma – Becci's and Matt's friend
Elliott – Matt's and Becci's friend

Prologue

I went in the afternoon to avoid seeing anyone – or being seen. It was two-ish, well before school finishing time. I walked. Mum wouldn't come – not that she was fit to drive a car anyway. I bought my flowers at the petrol station on the way. Two bunches of spray carnations wrapped in Cellophane – one pink, one yellow. Blue would have been too corny. They were a bit scabby and chewed-looking but there wasn't much choice – the man said there'd been a bit of a run on them. I'd have liked something more special – big expensive red roses or huge sunflowers maybe. Something more adequate. But it was the thought that counted. The gesture.

It was drizzling. Fine misty rain, the sort that seeps into all your clothes and makes you feel clammy. It was cold too, though not as cold as it had been at the weekend. The snow had pretty much all gone. There were just a few scraps of it in the gutter and along the bottom of the hedges – dirt-splattered and mingled with crisp packets and cigarette butts. I pulled my scarf up over my nose and mouth – partly to keep my ears warm, partly to mask my face.

The sight of the bus stop made me feel sick. They'd cleared away the broken glass and the debris but I could still see the marks on the road, like two black scars. And the bus shelter was leaning over perilously, all bent and buckled out of shape, its metal sides crumpled like a cardboard box someone had stamped on. I wanted to get the hell out but I made myself stay. It was the least I could do.

There were already loads of flowers. Some were on the bus-stop pole – their stalks lashed with masking tape or tied with string. Big juicy bouquets in fancy paper wrapping with ribbon bows and proper cards. 'Miss u', 'Sleep peacefully sweetheart', 'Luv u lots'. Someone had fastened a rugby ball there beside the lilies and chrysanthemums – a signed one, with Biro scribble fading in the rain. There were knick-knacks too – a teddy clutching a velvet heart tied to the pole with ribbon under its armpits, a Tigger toy, a photo of Brad Pitt.

There were more flowers laid on the pavement along the edge of the kerb – already tatty and dirt splashed – and still more fastened to the hedge a few feet back from the road. People had hung Christmas cards on twigs and wound tinsel in and out of the branches of the bushes. I saw a card that said 'It'll be lonely this Christmas . . .' with a sprig of mistletoe sellotaped to it. The card was damp and soggy and the writing had smudged but I recognised the signature. Friends – dozens of them. Mine and theirs. I pictured them filing to the site, flowers in hand – like pilgrims coming to a shrine. Weeping. Holding each other. Bringing their tape and string and scissors and carefully chosen tributes.

I hadn't thought to take string or tape so I poked the stems of my bouquets into the hedge as best I could. A strand of tinsel had blown away and snagged on some barbed wire. I tugged it free and threaded it around my flowers.

Light spills out onto the dark car park as the door swings open. Four friends step out into the cold, voices and laughter and the sound of a slow dance (*Mandy* by Westlife) tumbling in their wake.

'Oh wow! It's snowing!' says one of the girls – the one in the long white dress. She stretches out her hand, palm upwards to catch the flakes. With her pale moonlit face and black hair cascading down her back she looks like an ice queen. To her left, a strange couple descends the steps – he in a blue checked bathrobe, she in bunny ears and fishnet tights. 'God, it's cold,' the girl says. She shivers melodramatically and wraps her arms around herself. The boy opens his dressing gown and folds her into it, hugging her tight and kissing the tips of her rabbit ears. Behind them, another boy – or is he a man, all six feet four of him? – in a cumbersome yellow bird suit, like something off *Sesame Street*, takes the ice queen in a ballroom hold and waltzes with her towards the line of parked cars.

' "Oh-oh Man-dy! Well you came . . . and you gave

... without ta-a-aking ..."' He sings raucously, swinging her round in the snow.

'Car keys?' The boy in the dressing gown is trying to get his friend's attention. He stands beside a silver Vauxhall Corsa, the bunny-girl huddling against him for warmth. The boy in the bird suit is singing too loudly to hear so the boy in the bathrobe scoops a handful of snow from the thin powdering that is settling on the roof of the car and presses it together in his hands.

'Oi! Jefferson! Look!' he yells and the Big Bird lookalike spins round, his bulky costume silhouetted against the clubhouse lights. The snowball flies through the air and hits the yellow bird smack on the beak. 'Right!' he says, stooping to retaliate.

'Car keys?' says his friend again. 'I can't drive if you don't give me the keys. Hurry up – we're all freezing.' The boy in the bird suit stands up straight and starts to pat himself all over as if searching for pockets amongst his yellow feathers.

'Try *inside* the costume, goon,' says the ice queen. 'In your clothes!'

'I'm not wearing any clothes,' he says, 'only my boxers!' He grins and pauses to think. 'Damn, where *did* I put them?'

'You must have been wearing *something* when you arrived,' the boy in the bathrobe says. 'You didn't drive the car looking like *that*!'

'Jeans!' Big Bird says suddenly. 'I was wearing my jeans. I must have left them in the gents!' He turns and does a lumbering run back up the steps and in through the doors.

'What's he like?' says the other boy, jumping on the spot to keep warm.

Another blast of music escapes from the clubhouse as the yellow bird bursts back out into the car park holding a pair of jeans in one hand and a bunch of keys in the other.

' " . . . But I sent you a-wa-ay . . . Oh Man-dy!"' he sings as he waddles towards them. 'Catch!' He throws the keys to the boy in the dressing gown who catches them, points them at the car and plips the immobiliser switch. Side lights flash and the door locks snap up. Hastily, with more dramatic noises about how cold it is, the bunny and the ice queen and the boy in the blue checked bathrobe climb inside. They slam the doors shut and the boy starts the engine. Slipping the gears into reverse he backs quickly out of the space, flashing his lights at Big Bird, pretending he's going to drive off without him. Big Bird waves his arms in the headlights' beam and then, suddenly, without warning, dives onto the car bonnet and rolls across it like Starsky and Hutch.

'Don't go without me!' he shouts, pressing his beak against the cold windscreen and hammering with his fists.

The driver rolls down the window and hands his friend an ice scraper in the shape of Bart Simpson's face. 'You can knock the snow off the windows – seeing as you're already out there,' he says. 'I can't see a thing.'

'OK,' the bird says, 'but I don't need *that*!' Handing the ice scraper back, he turns to face away from the car and, pressing his big fat yellow ostrich bum against the car windows, starts to rub himself from side to side, wiping off the soft snow. Inside the car the others laugh as he swings his hips wildly, working his way, bit by bit around the car, like a belly dancer.

'OK, that'll do,' the driver says after a while. 'Don't milk it!'

The boy in the yellow suit opens the rear door on the passenger side and gets in beside the ice queen.

'Yuck! You're soaking,' she says as he puts his arm around her shoulders.

Slowly they pull out of the car park, passing three blokes in Elvis wigs all getting into a Ford Fiesta. They inch along the lane, past snow-covered rugby pitches, gleaming blue under the moon, and turn right onto Lowbrook Road, passing an outdoor Christmas tree decked with coloured lights like snooker balls. As the driver accelerates into fourth gear the girl with bunny ears leans across to switch on the radio.

Becci

There's no one in the water this morning except me. Often, when I swim before school, I have a whole lane to myself but today I have the whole pool. There's a lifeguard in a yellow T-shirt sitting on her ladder but she looks as if she's dozing. She hasn't moved for five whole minutes. I'm doing my usual eighty lengths – two kilometres, one and a quarter miles. Breaststroke. The water is deliciously smooth and flat and I can see every ripple I make. It slips through my fingers like blue silk. Steve, my coach, talks about 'stroke technique'. Stroking – that's what I'm doing. And that's what the water's doing to *me*. Stroking me . . .

Earlier this year I really needed to swim. It was the only time my brain switched off. I still have flashbacks – sounds, smells, sudden nightmarish images. Even when I'm thinking about something else, they crash in on me like those annoying pop-ups that appear on the screen when you're web surfing. But at the start the pictures were there all the time. My mind sifted through them relentlessly . . .

Swimming feels like a kind of hypnosis. The

rhythm of the strokes, the cool turquoise of the pool. Breathing ... and stretching ... and reaching ... and turning. Stroking. I count as I swim – count my strokes and count the lengths. And I watch the clock – check my times – see if a length is faster or slower than the one before. It's mindless. Boring. But it blanks things out.

Dad is in the foyer reading the paper when I come out.

'You were quick,' he says, tossing an empty vending-machine cup into the rubbish bin. 'Didn't you want to dry your hair?'

My hair hangs down in thick wet twists like tarred rope.

'I'll have a shower when I get home,' I say. 'The changing room is freezing.'

It's just getting light as we cross the car park. There are bands of luminous pink above the Leisure Centre roof. I zip my fleece right up to my chin.

'Feels like it might snow,' Dad says, unlocking the car.

'Will we still go?' I say. I close the car door and click on my seat belt.

'Yeah,' Dad says. He turns the ignition key, switches on the headlights, looks in the rear view mirror. 'I'll check the forecast, to be safe though,' he says as he backs out of the space.

On the way home, on Lowbrook Road, a cat crosses the road in front of us. Dad slows slightly when he sees it and it glances towards us, its eyes flashing like two jewels. Pop-ups again. *A fox with amber eyes shining in the headlights . . . Snow falling like torn paper . . . 'MIND OUT!'*

I run a bath instead of a shower because I'm cold and my body is aching. I fill it deep and lie back with my forehead and ears submerged, my hair waving underwater like a tangle of seaweed. I've just started shaving my legs when Dad knocks on the door.

'Emma's on the phone,' he says. 'Shall I say you'll ring her back?'

'Yep,' I say. 'Thanks, Dad.' I hook my foot behind the tap and run a bar of soap along my shin. The razor is a new one and ultra sharp. I nick myself just below the knee and a spot of blood leaks into the bath water, spreading like pink smoke. I think of Emma, wonder why she's ringing so early. Wonder if she's forgotten I'm not around today . . .

It was Emma's party we'd been to. Emma and Elliott's. Their birthdays are just two weeks apart so they decided to have a joint 'do'. It was at the Rugby Club. It was fancy dress – *themed* fancy dress.

'This is the deal,' Emma said, announcing it in the

Sixth-Form common room. 'You have to come as something beginning with E.'

'No way!' Matt said, stirring his Pot Noodle with a pencil.

Matt was never one for fancy dress. When we were kids he hated the whole dressing up and face painting thing. When it came to school plays he always wanted the parts where he could wear his ordinary clothes and look like he usually did. Like in the nativity play at Christmas – I would be a reindeer with antlers and a furry tunic and a big red nose, and Matt would be a carol singer with his coat on! Maybe a woolly hat if you were lucky.

People were pretty short on ideas at first.

'E?' Nathan said. 'That's a crap letter. Nothing begins with E!'

'Why *E*?' Dan Harris said. He was hitting the chocolate machine with his fist when he said it.

'Duh!' said Sophie. 'Because it's *E*-mma and *E*-lliot's party!'

'Egg,' said Elliott.

'Elephant' said Sophie.

'*Exactly*,' said Emma. 'Easy-peasy!'

If Matt was fancy-dress-a-phobic then Nathan was the other extreme. Any excuse for having a laugh and drawing attention to himself.

'Why don't you just go like *that*,' Matt said to him. They'd been having a jamming session – Nathan on electric guitar and Matt on bass – and Nathan was standing in our kitchen in his jeans, wiping sweat off his bare chest with a rolled-up T-shirt. '*Ex*-hibitionist!'

Nathan grinned and flexed his pecs. I was making toast in the background. I'd seen him without his clothes often enough – there are photos in our family album of me and Nathan stark naked in a paddling pool (not that I show them to many people these days!) – but he *was* looking pretty fit that day.

'Nah, I've rented a costume,' Nathan said. 'No expense spared. Wait till you see it . . .' He draped his soggy T-shirt round his shoulders like a boxer's towel and winked at me.

I went to Emma's party as an elf. Not a santa's-little-helper sort of elf but more the *Lord-of-the-Rings*-Liv-Tyler variety. I got some pointy ear extensions from the joke shop and a long white dress left over from when Mum was an angel in a play at church. I used straighteners on my hair so it was less bushy than usual and did mysterious make-up – pale with dark eyes and glittery cheekbones.

'You look great,' Mum said. 'Very elvish.' She was loading the dishwasher.

Matt came in from work and warmed up his lasagne in the microwave.

'I stink of pizza,' he said. Matt had been working weekends and Thursday nights at Pizza Piazza in town since he started in the Sixth Form. 'I need a shower,' he said, pinching the sleeve of his black T-shirt between finger and thumb and holding it up to his nose. (I'm sure Matt never used to wash so much before he started going out with Sophie.)

'Well hurry up eating, then,' I said. 'I'm ready. We don't want to miss all the action.'

'Only sad people get to parties early,' Dad said. He filled the kettle at the sink.

'Since when were you an expert on parties?' Mum said, patting his bottom as she passed him on the way to the fridge.

Matt sat down at the table and stared at me.

'Cher doesn't start with an E,' he said, scooping a forkful of food.

'Cher hasn't got pointy ears either,' I said, sticking my tongue out at him.

'What's Sophie going as?' Mum asked.

'Easter bunny,' said Matt, fanning his mouth to cool it.

'Cute,' I said.

'What about you?' Dad said.

'I'm going as Matt Fry,' he said, swigging down a glass of water.

'That's original,' said Mum.

'Wear my dressing gown and go as ET,' Dad said.

suddenly, pouring steaming water into the coffee pot.

'Nice one, Dad!' I said. 'Great idea.' He had this blue checked dressing gown that Grandma had bought him for Christmas. Dad's bald and short and when he first tried it on we all said he looked like ET.

'Too much hair,' Matt said, ruffling his shoulder-length locks.

'Oh make an effort, Matt,' Mum said, flicking him with a dish towel. 'You've got to go as *some*thing!'

So he went as ET – in a token costume – and spent the whole evening poking his finger out at people and saying 'Phone home!' when they couldn't work out what he was meant to be.

David

Matt and Becci got on well from the start – not like my brother's kids. (They're forever falling out – it's like a war zone in their house.) Maybe it helped that our two were close together in age. Becci's just fifteen months younger than Matt so we had our work cut out when they were babies – both of them in nappies and both still waking through the night. Sally and I are proud of the fact that they turned out to be good friends with each other, especially as they were always so different. Matt – very outdoorsy – climbing mountains, cycling, canoeing and so on. And of course Becci's a swimmer. Area Schools' Champion two years running.

When Becci started Sixth Form they had a lot of friends in common and hung around in the same gang, more or less. We were pleased. We had the sense that Matt would look out for Becci and make sure she didn't come to any harm. You worry about daughters more – which seems a bit ironic now.

I gave them both a lift to Emma's party, across town and out to the Rugby Club. It was a Saturday night in December – right at the end of a long term (almost anyway, just another three days of school after the weekend and then the Christmas holidays). I was feeling shattered and I had a streaming cold. I was happy to drive them, especially as it was a nasty night. But it felt as if I'd been doing overtime as 'Dad's Minicabs' recently – what with Becci's swimming every morning too. There seemed to have been a whole string of parties now that many of their friends were turning eighteen. (There's a great crowd in the Sixth Form – lots of youngsters who work hard and play hard. But then I'm biased. I'm very proud of the school.)

We were quite late setting off by the time Matt had had a shower and made himself smell nice. Becci was getting impatient as Matt faffed about with his fancy-dress costume. Not that it amounted to much. Becci had really pushed the boat out with Mr Spock ears and silvery lipstick. She looked like an extra from *Star Trek*. More Starship Enterprise than elvish but I didn't say so. Matt dressed up – grudgingly, I have to say – as the Extra Terrestrial. I lent him my dressing gown. It was an expensive one my mother had bought for me at John Lewis. I don't know what happened to it. I never asked . . .

We arrived at the party, and I parked in the Rugby Club car park. One of Matt's friends – a lad called Ben who plays keyboard in Matt's band

'Rootstrings' – walked past the car window in an Everton strip.

'Why is Ben dressed as a footballer?' Becci said.

'Everton fan!' Matt and I both said. We looked at each other and laughed.

Before they got out of the car, I gave Matt a tenner. 'Get a taxi,' I said, slipping it into his hand.

'Or he could always *Phone Home*!' Becci said.

'At two a.m.?' I said. 'Dream on. Some of us need our beauty sleep.'

'Some of us more than others,' Matt said with a grin.

'Have you got keys?' I asked. Becci fumbled in her bag.

'Yep,' she said. She leaned over to kiss my cheek. 'Don't wait up,' she said.

'Be good,' I said.

'Or if you can't be good . . .' Matt said, finishing the family saying, '. . . be magnificent!' He opened the car door and they were off, running towards the clubhouse in the drizzle.

I stopped off at Blockbuster Video on the way home and picked up a DVD to watch with Sally. She was supposed to have been working but a colleague had asked to swap shifts with her so we had a rare, unexpected night in. We lit a fire, put our feet up, opened a bottle of wine.

* * *

17

If only I'd gone back for them. If only they'd phoned for a taxi like I'd suggested. If only . . .

The 'if onlys . . .' drive you mad.

At the junction of Lowbrook Road and Millbank Lane a yellow gritting lorry indicates left and turns into the line of traffic in front of a silver Vauxhall Corsa. In the Corsa, the driver slows to ten miles an hour and changes down to second gear. Through the snow-spattered window he can see, in front of them, the gritter's amber light twirling, illuminating the hedges with its fiery glow. The girl beside him is singing along to a Coldplay song, her fishnet legs warm now in the hot wind of the car's heater.

In the back, directly behind the driver's seat, the girl in the long white dress takes a tube of Polo mints from her glittery handbag and tears it open with silver fingernails.

A truck comes towards them, headlights blazing, and passes by on the other side of the road. The driver, seeing nothing but blackness in the truck's wake, indicates right and pulls out into the centre of the road, accelerating to overtake the gritting lorry. As they pass it, particles of grit and salt spray up, peppering the sides of the car with shots like soft machine-gun fire.

'Sophie?' The rabbit girl glances round, her pink ears nodding as she turns her head. The girl with the Polo mints offers her the tube of sweets. 'Take one for Matt as well,' she says and the girl with rabbit ears takes two white rings. She holds them briefly in front of her eyes as if she is looking through a tiny pair of spectacles. Then she pops one into her own mouth and, reaching across the gear stick, she slips the other between the driver's lips just as he pulls left in front of the gritter and slows slightly, flicking his headlights onto full beam.

The snow in the car's headlights is fine now – more like rain. The girl with silver fingernails gives a mint to the boy in the yellow bird suit. He has slipped the head part of the costume backwards off his face now, like a hood, so that the beak is lolling against the nape of his neck. It looks weird – as if the bird is attacking him from behind. He smiles as he takes the Polo mint and the girl sees his eyes flash as a car passes in the opposite direction. She leans closer to him, wrapping her right arm across his furry bird belly and giggling as she squeezes his padding.

'Mind my feathers,' he says, stroking the back of her hair with his hand.

They pass the Leisure Centre, cloaked in total darkness, and turn left towards town. Here on the main road the snow is barely lying and the pavements glisten wet in the garish streetlamps.

The driver slows down, goes round a roundabout, passes the twenty-four-hour Tesco and the brightly lit windows of the Toyota garage. In the back seat the bird man is singing along to the radio. ' "Sex Bomb! Sex Bomb! You're my sex bomb! . . ."' He looks at the girl in the white dress nestled under his yellow wings as he sings and she smiles delightedly.

Just as they reach B&Q the girl in white turns her minty mouth towards him and he kisses her.

Becci

I'm standing in front of the bedroom mirror in a lilac bathrobe drying my hair. There's a photograph of Nathan Blu-Tacked to the edge of the mirror so I'm thinking about him. But then, when am I not?

Let me tell you about Nathan Jefferson . . . Where shall I start? I've known him pretty much since I was born – seventeen years. Sixteen anyway. But it goes back even further than that. Mum and Dad met Nathan's parents Stella and Mike when they were all at university in Nottingham. I think Mum actually went out with Mike for a while before she got it together with Dad, though she doesn't mention that much. Mike and Stella got married first and Dad was Mike's best man. (The photos are hilarious – Dad's still got hair!) Then Mike and Stella moved south and had three sons – The Jefferson Brothers, we called them. Meanwhile Mum and Dad had Matt, then me.

Before we lived in the same town as the Jeffersons we used to stay with each other for holidays. I always loved going to their house. It was noisy and they had football nets in the garden and banisters you could slide down. If it was summer we'd sleep in a big tent out the back and eat biscuits all night in our sleeping bags and play dares. One time we all went away together – all nine of us, plus the Jeffersons' dog, Monty. We rented a windmill in Norfolk right by the sea. I must have been six or so. I remember Nathan carrying me on his shoulders along a huge beach and Monty running out of the surf and shaking himself all over the picnic.

When Dad got a new job in the same town as the Jeffersons we were all delighted. I was ten when we moved. Nathan was thirteen. He'd just got an electric guitar and he was into Guns and Roses and Metallica.

Nathan was the middle brother of the three. Two years above him was Ben. Four years below was Jack. Nathan was always my favourite Jefferson – in fact he was *everybody's* favourite Jefferson. Even as a child he was huge – big flailing arms, big crashing feet, big wide grin. He always seemed to take up a lot of space, make a lot of noise, eat a lot of food. He was loud and sporty and outgoing – larger than life. Like Tigger.

I run a brush through my hair, coil the wet strands, point the nozzle of the hairdryer at them and stare at the snapshot of Nathan. It's a booth photo picture – just a small one. He's mucking about, putting his face too near the lens so his nose looks bulgy and distorted. I look at his big round eyes – note their look of perpetual amazement. I can see the scar on his eyebrow that he got playing rugby, like a white slash, dividing the line of hair like two words in a game of Hangman. It looks rugged and interesting. Why is it that boys' scars are considered handsome – desirable even, like fashion accessories?

His hair is blond in the picture – it must have been summer. In winter it was brownish – the same colour as Monty's fur – but when he'd been in the sun it went really light and his eyelashes turned white like Boris Becker's.

He's smiling in the photo – big wide froggy lips, teeth showing. Always when I think of him he's smiling.

What people liked about Nathan so much was his good humour. Ben's a bit of a stress-head and Jack can be moody and argumentative. But Nathan was consistently nice. Forever laughing. Nothing was a big deal. He was so laid back he was horizontal, as they say. He didn't even seem that bothered when he messed up his A levels. Nathan should have gone off to university last year – in the term Matt learned to drive – but instead he was having an unplanned 'gap year', working as a swimming pool attendant, strutting about in red shorts flashing his muscles at anyone who'd look! In January he was going to retake his Biology. Then in February he was planning to visit his uncle in Australia. He'd promised to bring me back a hat with corks on it like Crocodile Dundee . . .

Nathan and I were never really an item. Not properly. Not permanently. But I lived in hope. When we were little, the age gap seemed enormous. I was gawky and self-conscious and if Nathan thought about me at all I reckon it was only as a mate – or a sister-substitute perhaps. I had swimmer's shoulders and no bust and terrible acne. When I reached fifteen I looked slightly better – though I still had size eight feet and temperamental skin. I'd had a quiet crush on Nathan for years but it was only really when I got to the Sixth Form that he seemed to be getting the message that I fancied him. By then I was finally coming out of what Dad tactfully (not!) called my ugly duckling phase. Nathan was often at our house – or I was at his. He was in Matt's band for a while but he quit because he thought the stuff they played was too mellow! And of course he and Matt were mates – always had been. So we were around each other a lot.

Every now and then I'd catch Nathan looking at me as if he might be interested, or he'd cuddle me when we were sitting on the sofa watching TV, or suddenly start tickling me or something. But then he'd back off again and act really casual. I was never quite sure how he felt – and I never dared ask. Maybe he thought there was too much at stake, too much potential mess if things didn't work out. The end of a great friendship and all that. (Mum and Mike seem to have survived OK though so it's not as if you can't go back to being just friends.) But maybe the stark truth was he just didn't fancy me that much.

Looking at myself in the mirror now, that doesn't surprise me. I look ugly and pale and bulky. But then the last twelve months haven't exactly helped.

I switch off the hairdryer and tip my head upside down to try to fluff my hair up a little – make it less lank. I've had it cut since last Christmas. It isn't so long now and I've got a fringe so it covers my face more.

Nathan was even later getting to Emma's party than we were. He arrived in his mum's car, wearing his normal clothes and carrying two enormous carrier bags, and instantly disappeared into the toilets. He was ages in there. I hung around outside, trying not to look like I was hanging around outside the gents! When he eventually came out he looked like something from the Muppets.

'Ostrich?' said a bloke I didn't recognise. He was dressed as Dr Evil from *Austin Powers* and was helping himself to a handful of Doritos from a bowl on a table.

'Emu, please,' said Nathan.

The costume was amazing. It had a gigantic body with fluffy nylon feathers and Nathan's legs – which were in bright yellow tights (hairy legs showing through) – were poking out of the bottom like two sticks stuck in a lemon.

Protruding from the top of the body was a long elasticated neck like a tumble-dryer hose and at the end of that there was a feathery head with a massive orange beak. Nathan's face was peeping out of an oval window in the bird's neck about half a metre below the beak and there was a lever mechanism hidden inside the body that could make the neck go up and down so it looked as if the emu was pecking.

'Cool!' called Emma, walking off the dance floor towards us.

Matt came over with a bottle of Budweiser in his hand. 'That's a bit over the top, isn't it, Nath?' he said. 'Still, if you fail your resits you could always get a job on CBeebies!'

Nathan looked completely bizarre on the dance floor. I could hardly dance for laughing at him. He didn't *only* dance with me – he danced with lots of people – but he danced with me a lot. I was surprised. Delighted. It's not every day you get to dance with an over-sized yellow emu! The dance floor was heaving and there were so many overheated bodies that the windows were streaming with condensation. Nathan must have been roasting. There were rivers of sweat trickling down his temples.

'I'm dying of thirst,' he said, heading for the bar at the end of a Kylie number. He was drinking quite a bit – knocking back pints of lager like they were water.

'You could just take the costume off,' I said.

'No way,' Nathan laughed. 'Hiring it cost me thirty-five quid!'

When a slow dance came on later, I snuggled up close – which was tricky considering how big his belly was.

'Don't get too near,' he said, 'I bet I stink!'

'I'll live with it,' I said. 'There's nothing I like more than a rank-smelling ostrich – sorry, emu! Anyway, elves can't smell anything. It's part of the immortality thing.'

'Ah,' he said, looping his wings behind my back, 'you're supposed to be an elf? I thought you were that vampire from the Addams Family!'

'As if!' I said, cuffing him on the beak.

I got the mistletoe from Steph, a girl in my Business Studies group. She'd come dressed as an egg in a purple Humpty Dumpty costume but she'd abandoned the fancy dress halfway through the party in favour of a pair of jeans and a sparkly top. I'd bumped into her in the loos when she was changing out of the egg suit.

'Not much chance of pulling dressed like this,' she said. 'I mean did my bum look big or what?' I laughed.

'Did you have anyone in mind?' I asked, putting on lip gloss in the mirror.

'How do you mean?' she said, stuffing her costume into a bin liner.

'Pulling wise?' I said.

'Oh,' she said. 'Well, Elliott maybe . . .' She lifted a bunch of mistletoe out of her bag and shook it in front of my face.

'I feel a Christmas kiss coming on,' she said. 'Do you want a bit?' Steph broke the sprig in two and gave half to me.

'Bless!' I said.

Nathan was dancing with a big crowd when I came out of the loo. Matt and Sophie were with him. Sophie's ears had slipped a bit and Matt looked hot in Dad's dressing gown. They were dancing to *YMCA* – actions and everything. Most of the Sixth Form rugby team was there, including five lads dressed up as Emma – all in beanies with black braids made from strips of bin liner hanging out the bottom.

'Cheeky sods,' Emma said when she realised they were meant to be her.

Matt's drummer Pete and his friend Jez were in normal clothes but Pete had an 'Exit' sign hung round his neck and Jez had a sign that said 'Entrance'.

'Where did you nick those?' Matt said.

'Aldi car park!' Pete shouted above the music.

Nathan was really camping it up doing the actions. His emu head had flopped back so that his face was exposed and his floppy hair was all damp round the edges. He flashed me a big smile when he saw me that made me feel ten feet tall. It must have been that that made me do it . . .

At the end of the track I walked straight up to him, stood on tiptoe with the mistletoe in my hand and kissed him. It was the first time I'd ever kissed him properly and I only ever kissed him twice more. Once more at the party, in the corridor outside the gents toilet! And once in the car.

The Vauxhall Corsa comes to a halt at traffic lights on Western Road. There are few other cars about and most of the houses are in total darkness. On the glistening road, red light spills like a sprawling flower.

'I wonder how your mum's getting on with Arnold Schwarzenegger,' the driver says, looking across at the girl in bunny ears.

'Arnold Schwarzenegger?' says Nathan from the back seat.

'Sophie's mum's been out on a date with some bloke with a fake tan she met at salsa dancing!' says the girl in the long white dress.

'He looks like that bloke on the Cuprinol advert – the one with the wooden face!' Sophie says with a giggle.

'Ugh!' Nathan says, rearranging his long yellow legs.

Sophie looks out of the passenger window, running her finger across the misted-up glass.

'Is that Easter egg real?' says Nathan suddenly. On her knees, Sophie is cradling a woven basket with rope handles out of which peeps a foil-wrapped egg.

'Yep,' says Sophie without looking round.

'Where did you get an Easter egg in December?' Nathan says, shuffling in his seat.

'It was left over from last Easter. I hadn't got round to eating it yet!' Sophie says, twiddling the handles between her finger and thumb.

'No way!' Nathan says. 'That's months ago! Chocolate doesn't last ten minutes in our house . . .'

'He's right,' Matt says, slipping the gear stick into first as the lights turn amber. 'They're all greedy buggers. And the dog's the worst of the lot!'

'Do you remember that time just before Christmas when your mum left the wardrobe door open and Monty ate three selection boxes in one go?' the girl in white says.

'I bloody do!' Nathan says, running his fingers through his hair. 'She'd hidden them from us. He ate all the wrapping paper too!'

'Was he sick?' Sophie says.

'Nah, but he should have been,' Nathan says.

The car is accelerating now, pulling away from the lights, passing Kwik-Fit and PC World.

'Aren't you planning to eat it then?' Nathan says.

'What?' Sophie says.

'The Easter egg,' Matt says, glancing at her with a grin. 'Cos if you're not . . . we'll eat it for you!' Matt looks over his left shoulder and winks at Nathan whose face – diagonally opposite him – is dappled with shadow from streetlamps shining through the wet sunroof.

Sophie laughs and pulls the shiny egg out of the basket.

'It's probably past its sell-by date,' she says. 'You might get food poisoning . . .'

'We'll take the risk,' Nathan says, sitting forward in his seat.

'What was inside it?' Matt says.

'Smarties,' says Sophie. 'I ate those.'

'Shame,' says Matt.

'It's a bit warm and melty,' Sophie says, holding the egg in her cupped hands and squeezing it. 'I've been carrying it round with me all night.'

'Just stop teasing us and open it,' Matt says. The windscreen wipers are dancing like maniacs on the glass. The drizzle has eased now and the rubber blades on glass, barely damp, make an annoying squeaking sound. Matt flicks the switch to slow them down.

Sophie begins to unwrap the chocolate egg. Taking the foil off in one careful sheet she spreads it on her thighs and starts to break up the chocolate shell. Becci leans across Nathan's legs and reaches through the gap between the front seats to take a piece of chocolate off Sophie's lap.

'Quality control,' she says as she pops it in her

mouth. She sucks for a moment staring at the ceiling then she says, 'It's fine.'

Matt is heading for the town centre on the inner ring road. Someone in a Golf Gti speeds past him, overtaking recklessly just as they reach a bend.

'Tosser,' says Matt, watching the driver's tail lights disappear from view.

Sophie hands round the shards of Easter egg. Nathan and Becci, side by side in the back seat, eat in silence. Matt reaches another set of traffic lights just as they turn orange. He slows the car down, slips the gears into neutral, pulls on the hand brake.

Sophie stretches out her hand and puts a piece of chocolate into Matt's mouth. The chocolate has melted onto her fingers. She holds the tips of them in front of his lips momentarily and Matt licks off the chocolate. Then he leans towards her and kisses her mouth. The lights turn green but Matt doesn't notice.

'Oi!' says Nathan, with fake crossness. 'Concentrate on the road. Go!'

With one seamless motion Matt takes his left hand off Sophie's knee, flicks two fingers at Nathan in the back seat and puts the car into first gear with a rev of the gas.

Becci

Matt and Sophie had been seeing each other for just under two months. To mark their one month anniversary he'd bought her a single red rose – which Mum said was romantic and Dad said was a bad move.

'You're setting a precedent, Matt,' he said. We were sitting in the kitchen eating a takeaway curry. 'A rose for every month you go out with her – it'll get expensive. This time next year . . . you'll be looking at twenty quid, at least!'

'I'd better dump her now then,' Matt said, dipping a piece of naan bread into a foil dish of chicken tikka. He grinned at me across the table.

I don't know if he was planning to buy her two red roses when the end of December came around but he probably was, knowing Matt. He's always liked giving presents. In fact he'd bought Sophie's Christmas present the day of the party.

'I got it at lunchtime,' he said. 'While I was on my break.'

I was sitting on his bed watching him spraying Lynx under his armpits, wishing he'd hurry up before the night was half over. There was a small blue carrier bag from H Samuel on his bedside table.

'Have a look,' he said. He took a shirt out of the wardrobe, buttoned it in the mirror.

'I thought you were going as ET,' I said. I slid a small burgundy-coloured box out of the plastic bag.

'Yeah, but I've got to wear something underneath,' Matt said. 'I'm not going naked in a bathrobe!'

I opened the box, prising apart the hinged lid. 'Do you think she'll like it?' Matt said. It was a silver necklace. A heart on a chain. Simple. Delicate. Not really my taste but I thought Sophie would like it OK. It looked quite expensive.

'It's lovely,' I said. 'I'm sure she'll love it.' Matt was unbuttoning his shirt and staring into the wardrobe again.

'Wrong shirt,' he said, chucking the first shirt onto the bed.

'Oh hurry up, Matt!' I said. I looked in his mirror. Pouted at myself. Took my elvish lipstick out of my handbag and applied another coat.

'I'm sure she'll think you're gorgeous whatever you're wearing.' I said *gorgeous* in a sarcastic voice because it's weird when one of your mates suddenly thinks your brother is a sexy desirable hunk.

I look at myself in the mirror now. My eyes are a bit red from the chlorine in the pool. I put on some eye make-up. Rummage in my jewellery box for some earrings. Find the ones Matt bought me two Christmases ago.

I suppose it was down to me that Matt and Sophie got together in the first place. In actual fact I was a bit slow to see it coming. Sophie wasn't really his type. In the past Matt had always tended to fall in love with girls that were way out of his league – the glamorous ones that operate like magnets in the Sixth Form common room. The ones who'd never notice him, Matt Fry – floppy, dishevelled brown hair, cosy jumpers, nice but unremarkable face – in a million years. Sophie was small and quiet and pretty-ish, in a kind of fragile, pale, china doll sort of way. The type of face that on a good day looked lovely but on a bad day looked pallid and like her eyes were too big. He wasn't *her* type either. As far as I knew Sophie liked blonds – or more precisely, Brad Pitt and Justin Timberlake. I suppose Matt Fry was more readily available than either of those two.

We were never best mates, Sophie and I, but we were friends and we hung around in the same gang from about Year Nine onwards. A group of us used to go round to her place for girlie sleepovers. Sophie lived with her mum, Kirsty – just the two of them. Kirsty was a laugh. She'd paint our nails for us – mad designs and sparkly bits – and let us cook stir-fry noodles in the middle of the night. I used to really like Sophie's mum back then. Before she started being such a cow to Mum. Before she took to ringing her up and screaming at her down the phone . . .

I suddenly saw a lot of Sophie in the summer after GCSEs, partly because Emma was away in Jamaica for a couple of months with her grandparents. Sophie started coming round to our house more frequently than she'd done before. She often seemed to come when Matt's band were rehearsing – appearing out of the blue when they were having a break and making Pop Tarts in the kitchen or drinking beer in the back garden. We'd join them, like a pair of groupies. Sophie seemed unusually interested in their music, even though it wasn't that good. Once she asked me if I thought Matt would let her be a backing vocalist if they played a gig. I thought she was joking but she wasn't. 'Ask him, Becci,' she said. I said I would but I didn't. He'd have said something dismissive like 'It's not R and B, Becci!' But then maybe he wouldn't have. Maybe he'd have jumped at the chance.

When we started in the Sixth Form Sophie signed up for the Duke of Edinburgh Award Scheme, which struck me as odd – a bit out of character. Call me thick but it didn't dawn on me that she'd only done it so she'd get rock climbing tuition from Matt. Then she started doing Law A level – the same as Matt – and she kept ringing him up to ask for help with homework.

'It's Sophie,' Mum would shout up the stairs.

'For me?' I'd say, stepping out onto the landing.

'No, for Matt,' Mum would say. 'Knock on his door, would you?'

I finally tumbled to the fact that she liked him when she asked me one day whether Matt had a hairy chest. She was sitting on my bed reading a magazine article with lots of photos of celebrity chests – Brad's and Justin's included.

'My God, you fancy him, don't you!' I said.

'Duh!' she said, going mildly pink.

It was less than a week after that that they got it together. We were at the Sixth Form Icebreaker, which is a big 'do' in a nightclub in town where everybody is supposed to get to know each other. (All the teachers stand around with drinks in their hands trying to look cool – even though they're the same dull teachers you've had since you were eleven!)

Anyway, that was when it happened. Halfway through *Rock Your Body* by Justin Timberlake, if you want the precise moment.

It's strange when your friend tells you that your brother is a good kisser. There are some things that you'd actually rather not know . . .

* * *

Suddenly I notice the time. I'm still in my lilac bathrobe and, as I can't find anything to wear in my drawers, I go downstairs. Mum is at the kitchen table with a blank face, eating bran flakes – dry – straight from the packet in handfuls. I pick up the phone and dial Emma's number . . .

Emma

It's my birthday again soon. I'm going to do something really quiet this year. No big 'do'. No fancy dress. I suppose I feel bad that it all happened after my party – as if it was somehow my fault.

Mr French, our headteacher, announced it in the Sixth Form assembly on the Monday morning. Some people didn't know by then, which makes you wonder where they'd been all weekend. There was an audible gasp at the news and then several girls started crying really noisily.

Normal school kind of disintegrated for a day or two – maybe more so because it was the end of term anyway. They brought in counsellors that people could go and see if they were upset and they put a book of remembrance in the library that you could go and write messages in. There was a huge queue to get to it all through the lunch hour. To be honest, I reckon some people went a bit over the top. I mean I know they were popular – don't get me wrong – but there were kids who hardly knew them crying on each other's shoulders in the corridors. What's that all about?

Loads of us put flowers at the place where it happened, by the road. That's fair enough. You feel like you want to do *something*. But there was a great stack of flowers at the school gates too. In the end Mr French had to ask people to stop bringing any more because they were blocking the pavement and the path was getting slippery with all the petals and stuff.

We had a special assembly on the Wednesday. Whole school. More sobbing. Mr Fry wasn't there – obviously.

Becci

Dad teaches at our school. When I started in Year Seven he was just a physics teacher. Then he became Head of Lower School. Now he's Deputy Head. He and Mr French are a bit of a double act – French and Fry – so there are lots of jokes about French Fries. (Ho ho.) Dad's the one who sorts out trouble-makers – the one you get sent to if you're pratting about. That was a bit weird for Matt and me at first but you get used to it. It helps that Dad – Mr Fry – is quite popular. Kids like him, on the whole. They think he's strict but funny. He's a great storyteller and he does very entertaining assemblies. It would be much worse for us if he was boring. Or a plonker . . .

When it happened, Dad had the last three days of term off. Then we had two weeks' holiday. But then January came and Dad went back to work pretty much as normal. People commented on how strong he was. How well he was coping. How brave he was to hold it together.

Nathan's dad, Mike, was the same. He works with

computers and he travels about a lot. After he'd had a couple of weeks off over Christmas he was back on the road again. Full time. Full on. I wonder if that's a man thing . . . that you keep going, as if nothing's changed?

Mum was the opposite. She cracked up completely. Maybe that's because of the job she does. She's a radiologist in the X-Ray department of A and E – so she deals all day long with people who've had accidents. Bleeding people. Broken people. She just couldn't do it any more. She'd get as far as the hospital car park and have to come home again. Or she'd never leave the house. Ring in sick. They gave her time off work – called it post-traumatic stress – recommended that she have some counselling. She sat at home and watched daytime TV and ate a lot and got fat. She's three sizes bigger than she used to be and she wears shapeless stretchy clothes from Matalan. 'I have good days and bad days,' she says, if anyone phones to ask how she is.

Today looks like a bad day. I put down the telephone receiver (Emma's number's engaged . . .) and walk into the kitchen. Mum's still wearing the old T-shirt and leggings she wears as pyjamas and she's got bed-head hair. I lift the ironing basket down off the top of the washing machine and start rummaging in it for something to wear. Mum doesn't speak. I find a crumpled pair of jeans and a top. Set up the ironing board. Switch on the iron. An orange light comes on with a click.

While the iron is heating up I walk across to Mum. I wrap my arms around her shoulders where she's sitting and give her a hug. Her scalp smells like cheese.

'Love you,' I say, squeezing her, and her eyes brim with tears.

The silver Corsa is going through town on the inner ring road now, snaking through the one-way system. Just by Argos and John Lewis it stops at lights. In the passenger seat, Sophie presses her index finger into the last few crumbs of chocolate on the Easter egg foil and puts her fingertip in her mouth. Matt checks his mirror, pulls away as the lights turn green, turns right at River Island.

'I'm starving,' Nathan says from the back seat.

'No, you're just a greedy bastard,' says Matt. He smiles at Sophie, glances in his mirror, changes gear. At the next junction they give way – slow to a halt for a moment – just outside Pickin Chickin. Lights blaze out through steamed-up windows and the smell of fried food wafts towards the car.

'Chips!' Nathan says, enthusiastically. 'Stop the car! I need chips!' Matt grins and pulls into a parking space on the left-hand side. He switches off the engine. Nathan opens the back door and the courtesy light comes on, illuminating three faces.

'You're not going like *that*?' Becci says, nodding at his emu suit. Nathan plays dumb, 'Like *what*?' he says. He steps out onto the pavement, his yellow legs ridiculous in the streetlights. 'Anyone else want chips?' he says. Nobody answers. The car radio has gone crackly. Sophie tunes it to another station. They catch the tail end of a Destiny's Child song.

Through the nearside window Becci watches Nathan open the door of Pickin Chickin and walk into the garish red interior. Beyond the misted glass she sees him ordering, gesticulating with his wings to the pictures of food on the restaurant wall. She sees the man behind the counter – stripy top, cheesy red baseball cap – laugh and point to Nathan's costume. On the inside of the window are food prices, written in red vinyl lettering that is peeling away. *Po tion f chips . . . battere cod . . . quart r hicken . . .* and a cartoon image of a big fat smiling chicken.

'Spot the similarity,' says Matt – looking through the window and seeing Nathan's emu body alongside the grinning chicken. Nathan is patting himself again – the way he did when he couldn't find the car keys. Now he's coming out empty-handed, walking towards the car.

'I bet he hasn't got any money,' says Becci. Nathan taps on the glass and Sophie rolls her window down.

'Can you lend me some cash?' he says sheepishly.

Matt reaches into his jeans, takes out his wallet, hands Nathan the tenner his dad gave him for a taxi.

'Here,' he says with a fake sigh. 'Get me some too,

seeing as though I'm paying!' Nathan goes back inside the shop and the man in the red cap starts wrapping chips, shovelling them out of the deep fat fryer onto the paper.

Sophie shivers. 'I'm SO cold,' she says. 'Look!' She breathes out with a 'huh' sound and a cloud of steam appears in front of her. Matt starts the engine again and turns up the heater full blast so it hums noisily. 'Thanks,' she says. She wraps her arms across her chest and hugs herself.

'Have this,' Matt says. He lifts his bottom off the driver's seat and starts wriggling his arms out of the bathrobe. Behind him, Becci reaches over the back of his seat and tugs the dressing gown free where it's caught underneath him. Matt wraps the blue dressing gown round Sophie's shoulders, kissing the tip of her nose as he does so.

'Bless!' says Becci from the back seat.

Nathan is at the window again with two parcels of chips. Becci leans across and opens the rear passenger door from the inside.

'Hurry up,' Matt says. 'We're all dying of hypothermia.'

Nathan climbs in, ducking his head in at the door. 'Chips with salt and ketchup for Matt,' he says, reaching across with a warm, greasy parcel. 'And chips with curry sauce for me. Cheers, Matt.'

Matt cradles the packet of chips on his lap, revs

the engine, puts it into first gear and pulls out of the parking space, glancing over his shoulder as he goes.

Becci

I take my ironed jeans and top – still warm, folded across my arm like a waiter's towel – and go back upstairs. When I'm dressed, I pull the curtains. It's light now, but only just. The sky is a thick yellowy white – like whipped cream – and it's beginning to snow. I watch the flakes coming down in slow motion, sticking to the glass, then slipping, melting. This is the first time it's snowed this year. The first time since the night of Emma's party.

I used to love snow. Matt and I would play in it – make snow holes and snowmen. Where we used to live it snowed much more than it does here. And where my grandparents live, in Scotland, it snows loads, in big deep drifts like sand dunes. There's a great hill behind their house where we used to sledge. Grandpa had this fantastic old sledge with curved wooden slats and metal runners. It was just big enough for Matt and me to ride together – me on the front, Matt on the back with his legs either side of me. When I was little it would make me feel really safe, Matt sitting behind me, arms around my waist. With our combined weight we'd go like the wind.

Grandpa always insisted we dry the runners after we came in from the snow and polish them with linseed oil on an old rag to make them shine. I used to think they were made of silver they shone so much.

Now snow makes me feel uneasy. I notice this knotted feeling appearing in my stomach – like a lump of something growing inside me. I feel cold, despite my hot bath ... I touch the radiator underneath my windowsill to see if it's on and it's boiling – so hot, I flinch my fingers away. I look in the drawer under my bed to find something cosy to wear over my top but I can't find anything. So I go into Matt's room.

Matt's room is exactly as it always was. Blue walls, bare floorboards, blue and green striped rug. IKEA duvet cover – blue and green checks. Big green squashy cushion with ink stains from when his fountain pen leaked. Lava lamp by the bed – switched off. White chipboard desk – with compass grooves along the edge where he fiddled when he got bored doing his homework. Silver anglepoise light. Aluminium mesh waste-paper basket – empty. Against the far wall, pine bookshelves – full, apart from the odd gap where the books lean like pieces of broken fence. *Criminal Law, Blackadder, the Complete Scripts Series One and Two, Tony Benn – Diaries, Introduction to Psychology, Lord of the Flies, Cardiff University Student Prospectus, Touching the Void, Lake*

District Walks, *The Little Book of Calm*, *Bart Simpson's Guide to Life*, ... I scan my eyes along the books' spines. Beside the books there's another shelf of CDs – Jimmy Hendrix, Bob Marley, Red Hot Chili Peppers, Moby, Coldplay, Radiohead, Aqualung. Above the desk is a cork noticeboard with bits and pieces pinned to it – last year's Sixth Form timetable, an out-of-date book token, a postcard of Ben Nevis, mobile numbers scrawled on scraps of paper, a pencil doodle of a squirrel riding a unicycle! I notice that the photo of Sophie isn't there any more.

Opening the wardrobe door I see Matt's clothes hanging there – silent and unnaturally tidy. I touch the sleeve of a shirt, run my fingers across a pair of jeans. Close the wardrobe door. Catch sight of myself in the mirror by the door. Look away.

To the left of the mirror is Matt's bass guitar, leaning on its stand, all glossy and black. I remember how annoying I used to find it when he was practising – the same riffs over and over again, reverberating round the house.

Above the guitar there's another shelf – his 'Glory Shelf' we used to call it. Trophies – for football and canoeing and music – and certificates, in frames. Boys' Area District Long Jump Champion. Duke of Edinburgh's Gold Award. Bass Guitar Grade 8. Certificate of Mountain Leadership. Boy with

Bushiest Eyebrows – that one was a joke (obviously). Nathan made it.

I suppose it's fair to say I've always felt a bit in Matt's shadow. He's always done better at school than me. Always achieved more. Always given Mum and Dad more obvious satisfaction. Always had more strings to his bow. When he applied to university his UCAS personal statement was three pages long!

I sit on Matt's floor for a moment – with my back against the side of the bed. Running my palms along the polished boards, I look at the posters on the walls – photos of bands, Lisa Simpson impersonating Munch's *The Scream*, the Himalayas at sunset, Cameron Diaz leaning against a tree . . . I look at the clay figure Matt made in GCSE art of a woman kneeling. He drew Mum before he modelled it. I remember him asking her to kneel on the living room floor – Mum getting irritable because it was taking too long and she had stuff to do. It was a really good drawing. It looked just like her. Or rather, like she used to look.

I used to think it was a pisser that Matt was good at art on top of everything else. It felt like he got all the talents and I got none – like something went a bit wrong with the distribution process, like the portions weren't quite fair. When I think things like that now I hate myself for being so mean-spirited. How can I feel jealous of him now?

I stand up and look out of the window. The snow is coming down more heavily and I notice it's lying on next door's garage roof. Beside the window, to the right of the curtains, hanging on a hook, is Matt's climbing harness and a length of purple nylon climbing rope, immaculately coiled. I find myself wondering who coiled it like that? Did Matt do it? Last time he used it? Or was it Mum – trying to make the place look tidy? Precise. Holding back the tide of mess.

Glancing round Matt's bedroom, everything looks *too* neat. That's the thing I notice most, when I come in here. My first impression. There are no boxer shorts on the floor, no damp towels left in heaps, no crisp packets under the bed, or hairs, or nail clippings – all the stuff Mum used to nag Matt about. It all looks orderly. Orderly and soulless.

I'm standing in the middle of the floor now, staring round me. For a moment I've forgotten why I came in. Then I remember. I open the bottom drawer in Matt's chest of drawers and take out a big grey jumper. It's one that Grannie Fry knitted a couple of Christmases ago. We called it Matt's 'Poodle Jumper'. It's flecky like a beach pebble and sort of loopy and bobbly. I unfold it and pull it over my head. It feels fluffy and soft. I fold the polo neck up round my nose and mouth like a bandit's mask and let the sleeves come down over my hands like dangly gloves. The wool around the collar smells of Matt. It's an earthy, oily smell – quite subtle. Probably, I'd never have noticed it when he was here . . .

Suddenly I miss him with a terrible ache.

Sally

I was going to go with Becci and David today. That was what we decided, before we all went to bed last night. Becci said it would mean a lot if I went and that it might make me feel more positive. I said I'd do it for her. 'Do it for Matt,' she said. She was sitting at the other end of the sofa from me, massaging my feet. She'd stayed in to keep me company, even though it was a Friday night. She hardly goes out these days – apart from school and swimming. I worry that life's not much fun for her any more . . .

I felt pretty good when I went to bed but then I slept badly and woke up feeling fragile and disorientated. I got up and made a cup of tea and I knew I couldn't face the trip. Some days my skin just feels too thin. The slightest little thing upsets me. Like when Becci gave me a hug at the breakfast table. She did it to make me feel nice, but instead it just made me cry.

David thinks I should cope better with everything. He doesn't say so – he's too kind and tactful – but I know he thinks it. I can tell by the look on his face. He's trying to be patient but secretly he wants to give me a good slap. He thinks I dwell too much on things. That I need to move on a bit. Think of the future. Focus on all the positives. I bet he'd like to give me a motivational chat like he gives his students at school – set me a few targets and objectives.

I *did* go back to work a few months ago. I'd had several months off and I thought I was ready for it. I work in A and E – Casualty – in Radiology. I coped all right for a while. Broken arms and legs weren't a problem, and sprained wrists and dislocated elbows. Even head injuries were OK provided there wasn't too much blood. It was the major stuff I couldn't deal with. Trauma. Damage.

I used to be able to cope with anything. It was just a job. It didn't get to me. I didn't let it. But now ... it's too close to home. They're not just accident victims any more. They're people with families. With mothers. I'd find myself breaking down – cracking up like a bad radio signal. Becoming incapable of looking people in the eye. Incoherent. Unable to string a sentence together. That's not fair on patients. People need reassuring when they come to hospital. They don't need some daft middle-aged woman weeping over their X-ray photographs.

Anyway, I'd only been back at work a fortnight when there was a bad traffic incident out on the bypass. Four under-twenty-ones in a head-on smash. One was dead on arrival, two were critical – one with severe head and spinal injuries, one with a crushed pelvis. The ambulance phoned through to say they were bringing them in and I had a panic attack. I got all short of breath and shaky and nauseous. My manager sent me home, even though she was chronically short-staffed – which was incredibly nice of her.

Some people have been *so* nice – so very kind. Others have been unbelievably cruel . . .

I fold down the tops of the cereal packets and stash them carefully in the cupboard. Then I wipe up some splashes of milk from the kitchen table and squash an empty milk container into the swing-top bin. I pull the cord to lift the blinds and let some light into the kitchen. Becci has left the iron on – it hums and spits as it stands upended on the ironing board. Mechanically, without thinking too much, I switch it off, unplug it, lift it onto the worktop to cool. Then I turn off the light and go upstairs to take a shower.

In the bathroom, I look at myself in the mirror. I have a lot more grey hairs than I had this time last year. And my face is fatter. I look as if I've been pumped up – inflated to fill my skin. Some mornings I think I look like an old woman. David routinely, dutifully, tells me I look nice – but I know he's lying.

* * *

I should have been working the night it happened. I was scheduled for a late shift. I should have been the one standing by to X-ray them, the one that took the call from the ambulance crew. I've dreamt about that happening several times now. Every time I wake up sweating.

Debbie, my colleague, asked to swap with me so she could go to her nephew's birthday party in the afternoon. So, in the end, I came off duty at six o'clock and she did the six till four. Maybe if I *had* been working David would have gone back to collect them instead of falling asleep in front of the fire . . .

I hear the creak and slam of the garage door as it clatters open. Then I hear the car engine roar into life and the gears crunch as David reverses out onto the drive. Becci is running downstairs. I hear the thud of her feet.

'Bye, Mum!' she shouts. Cheerful. Forgiving.

'Give him my love,' I say feebly as I turn on the shower.

Becci

Dad's reversing out onto the road as I shut the front door behind me. I trot down the drive and, in the short time it takes me to reach the car, Matt's grey jumper gets peppered with snowflakes. I climb into the passenger seat, put on my seat belt, wipe a splash of snow from my forehead with the back of my hand. I'm wearing my stripy scarf and grey gloves with no fingers and I still feel cold.

'Are you sure you want to go?' I say, glancing in the wing mirror and pushing my hair out of my eyes.

'Yeah,' says Dad. 'But we won't stay long. It'll be fine. The motorway will be clear. It isn't really lying. The ground's too wet . . .' That's so typical of Dad. Always the optimist. Always assuming things will work out for the best. Nothing's ever as bad as it seems . . . I used to find that so reassuring when I was small.

But as we pull off along our road I can't help noticing how thick the snow is getting. And it *is* lying – whatever Dad says. It's settling on the grass verges and trees that line the street like a dusting of sugar. I sit back in the chair and try to relax – try to push down the mounting sense of panic that the snow triggers. I look hard at my grey woollen sleeves – focus on the melting ice crystals – the way they're disappearing, leaving only dampness behind them.

'I need petrol,' says Dad. He pulls out of the end of our road, negotiates the mini-roundabout, heads towards Waitrose. Turning into the supermarket car park he heads for the petrol pumps, pausing at the recycling bins to post a couple of empty wine bottles through the rubber lips of the slot. I hear them clash. Broken glass. Flashbacks again.

'I won't be a minute,' I say. 'I just want to get some sweets and stuff. I'll catch you up . . .'

I jump out of the car, pull my scarf up over my ears and run across the car park, threading my way past snow-capped cars and Saturday shoppers. I head towards the automatic doors. Just inside the door, under a tinsel banner, someone dressed as Rudolph the Red Nosed Reindeer is collecting for charity. The reindeer reaches out a fur covered arm and rattles his tin at me. I stop, too embarrassed to walk past, and fumble in my pocket for a fifty pence piece.

'Bless you!' he says – too jovial for this time in the morning (someone should tell him!). As my coin clatters through the slot, Rudolph presses a button on his antlers which kick-starts a tinny version of *Jingle Bells*.

'Merry Christmas!' he says. Hasn't he noticed that he's a month too soon?

I scurry away, snatch up a wire basket and head for the confectionery aisle. Into my basket I put a Crunchie, a Boost bar, a King Size Dairy Milk, a bag of Maltesers and two tubes of wine gums. Then I make my way along the drinks aisle and pick up a four bottle pack of Dr Pepper. As I go through the fruit and veg section on my way to the checkout I pass a display stand (more Christmas decorations) piled high with nuts and satsumas. On impulse I pick up a bag of satsumas – feel their cool fleshy skins through the red string netting – drop them into my basket. They're a token stab at healthiness – to offset all the chocolate. And they're irresistibly cheery. Comfort food for cold days.

I go through the ten items or less checkout and pay for my goods – five pounds eleven pence. Seems a bit steep, but it's too late now. I shovel my eight items into a carrier bag – special Christmas version with sprigs of holly – and walk quickly towards the door.

As I'm going through the automatic doors I meet Stella. (Mrs Jefferson – Nathan's mum.) If I'd spotted her coming I might have darted sideways behind the magazine stall – turned my back and tried to look really interested in *Hello!* magazine – or even nipped into the loo. But as it happens we come face to face.

And she's smiling. She hugs me. Kisses me softly on the right cheek.

'Becci,' she says, delightedly. 'How are you?'

'Fine,' I mumble meaninglessly. Her cheek is still against mine. I can smell her perfume – the same one she's worn for years. She's wearing a denim jacket and a purple velvet scarf. Stylish as ever. She hasn't let herself go the way Mum has. I notice she's had blonde highlights put in her hair but apart from that she looks like she always does. Same luminous face. Same twinkly eyes.

'Hi,' I say. I try to smile too but I can't look her in the eye. Instead I look to the side of her, over her left shoulder. A man is coming towards us pushing a trolley with a squalling toddler in it. I see the furry reindeer shake his tin hopefully at the man with the trolley and the man with the trolley walk straight past him. It makes me want to laugh, but I hold it in. I raise my carrier bag by way of explanation.

'Dad's in the car,' I say, pointing vaguely towards the petrol pumps. 'We're just . . .' I don't finish my sentence.

Stella has started talking at the same time as me.

'Are you just off to . . .?' She doesn't finish her sentence either. She doesn't need to.

'Well,' I say, 'I'd better go.' I force a smile but I still don't look at her. I look at the ground – at the grimy tyre tracks in the snow, the muddy wetness around my shoes.

'Nice to see you,' Stella says. She says it to my back because I've already started to walk away. If I stay any longer I know I'll melt – just like the snowflakes on my sweater. Matt's sweater.

'Give my love to . . .' I nod '. . . everyone,' I hear her say.

Dad has the radio on in the car when I get back. Radio Two. Jonathan Ross. Dad's humming along to an Oasis song and eating a packet of cracked sea salt-and-black pepper crisps.

'Everything OK?' he says, offering the gaping mouth of the crisp bag to me.

'Fine,' I say, stowing my parcel of goodies at my feet. I shake my head in the direction of the crisps.

'You were ages,' Dad says, folding the foil bag in two and tucking it into the pouch in the side of the driver's door. I put my seat belt on with a clunk. Dad turns the ignition key and the engine roars into life.

'I met Stella,' I say.

Dad glances at me quickly, gauging my response, and I pretend not to notice. I look out of the window and say, 'Can we have Radio One?'

Dad puts the car in gear and pulls out of the snowy car park.

Stella

It really upset me, seeing Becci – threw me off my stride, knocked me sideways a little. It wasn't actually seeing her that got to me. (The truth is I'd love to see more of her, love her to come round and chat like she used to. Sit at my kitchen table and leaf through recipe books and bake brownies and prattle about who did this and who did that and who said what to whom . . . you know, girl stuff!) No, it was the way she reacted. The way she wouldn't look at me. The way she wriggled free when I embraced her – spoke no more than half a dozen words. It was as if she'd screened herself off from me in some way – as though she was locked behind a sheet of perspex that I wasn't allowed to penetrate. Self-protection? I imagine so. In my experience it doesn't help – it just deadens you. Slows down the healing.

Sally's even worse than that – not that I've seen her for weeks. Months even? Before (everything falls into two compartments now, 'Before' and 'After') the four of us used to play badminton on Friday nights. We'd often go for a drink afterwards. Sometimes – as the kids got older – they'd come with us and we'd play pool or cards or *Simpsons Top Trumps*. Sally and I have been close friends for years. We had our babies together. We used to be able to talk about anything. Everything.

After, we still talked, for a while. Even when we didn't talk there was a sense of carrying each other's grief – pooling our collective pain in one deep black lake. Sharing it out. Just holding each other.

But then Sally withdrew. Maybe it was the blame. All the stuff in the papers. The things they said about Matt. And the court hearing. The recriminations – all those bile-laden letters. It took its toll on Sally and bit by bit she stopped communicating. Stopped answering the phone. Didn't return my calls. Didn't answer the door when I went round. It was as if she stepped into the deep freeze. Little by little she iced over. Froze. I know that's a perfectly normal reaction. But – bugger it – Sally's my friend. I need her! *I'm* sad too.

There I go, collapsing into self-pity . . . Sometimes, when I get like this I think she should be phoning *me*, that *I'm* the one that needs support, that *I've* suffered more than she has. But perhaps I haven't. Anyway, how can you quantify pain? Say that one person's grief is heavier than another's? It's not as if you can weigh it, or measure it . . .

* * *

Becci said David was in the car, waiting. I was a bit surprised they were making the journey in this weather. The forecast isn't great . . . I know Saturdays are hard for them. But they're hard for me too. I used to watch Nathan play rugby on Saturday mornings. I can't say I miss the rugby itself – all that unintelligible rolling around in the mud and the aggression and the over-competitive parents yelling at the ref and the fear that at any moment it might be *your* son with a broken neck. And I certainly don't miss the mess afterwards – the filthy kit, the clods of earth dropping off his boots and shorts so muddy you could grow potatoes in them. The trail of dirty footprints to the shower and that smell of liniment that hung around his kit bag – sickly and medicinal . . . Actually I'm lying. I *do* miss all that. I just miss Nathan. I miss everything about him. I miss his smiles, his cataclysmic hugs, his crashing feet – even his explosive temper tantrums. (At least we've still got the hole in the bathroom door to remember him by – the one he punched one day when Ben was winding him up.)

People (even intelligent, sensitive, sensible people) think that when someone dies you don't want to talk about them. That it's somehow too difficult. That – as subjects for conversation – dead people are off limits. But I want to talk about Nathan *all the time*. I want to describe him, to recall him, to conjure him up with words and memories. Talking helps fill the space he's left behind . . .

I can feel myself unravelling. Soon I'll be weeping. Not that there's anything wrong with that. It's just it scares people . . .

The woman at the checkout is looking at me nervously as I shove lettuce and cherry tomatoes and yogurt and pasta into plastic bags. I take a deep breath, smile at her, hand over my Visa card.

When I get outside the snow has turned to drizzle and the car park is covered in pools of slush. The cold air hits my face as if it's slapping some sense into me. I make a conscious decision to stop thinking about Nathan – to step aside from grief for a while – to think not about my dead child but about my living children. My living, changing, needy, somewhat neglected children. So I think of Ben – coming home from university in a week or so. I picture him in Southampton in his poky flat with his bossy girlfriend. Remind myself to ring him tonight, to offer to pay his train fare home. To send him some new socks – he never has enough socks. What does he do with them? I suspect he throws them out instead of washing them.

Then I think of Jack – Jack with his black T-shirts and his skater hair and his monosyllabic friends with rank-smelling armpits . . . Jack who barely speaks to me – let alone hugs me. Jack who boils and seethes with resentment, who is embarrassed at my every action, my every gesture. So much for positive thinking. Why am I feeling so negative? So cynical? Oh sod it . . . I'm allowed to feel negative from time to time. I've lost a son. It's like having a limb amputated . . .

A man pulls out of a parking space without looking and almost crashes into my trolley. That's all I need. I swear audibly and then I start to cry. Bugger.

I'm halfway home when I remember my errand. I'm tempted to leave it – go another day – but Jack asks me for so little these days, and I can't face his acrimonious stare if I fail in my mission, so I double back and park in the multi-storey. At the skateboard shop, 'X-Treme', (more black T-shirts and body odour) I take a scrap of paper from my purse and read Jack's squiggly handwriting. He wants bearings – Lucky Sevens. Titanium. They come in a plastic tube, like camera film. I feel stupid and middle-aged asking for them – as if I'm speaking a foreign language and getting the accent all wrong. They are ludicrously expensive – but at least he isn't spending his pocket money on drugs. The man behind the counter – half my age, goatee beard, T-shirt that says 'Show us your tits!' – looks amused by me. Then suddenly I realise he's flirting with me, asking me if I'd like to try out one of his decks, check out some moves. I feel myself reddening as I fumble with my change, zip my purse, slip the plastic canister into my handbag. Despite the blushing and the slightly foolish feeling this little encounter brings on, I feel my mood lifting like the sun coming out after a long day of rain. But it's only temporary.

As I turn away from the counter, smiling smugly to myself, and start to leaf through the Airwalk T-shirts on the rail by the door, a song comes on the radio that shatters my fragile sense of well-being. It's Metallica. Loud and thrashing and sweaty. Nathan's favourite song. We played it at his funeral. I feel myself going to pieces so I leave the shop quickly, pushing past a gang of teenage boys trying on hoodies. When 'Show us your tits!' shouts 'See you again!' I don't answer.

We played the song right at the start of the service – as they brought Nathan's body into the church. My mother was shocked. What did she expect? Faure's *Requiem*? He was eighteen! Six of Nathan's friends carried the coffin. Matt wasn't one of the six – obviously – but by rights, he should have been. In some ways, Matt and Nathan were more like brothers than mates. They'd criticise each other and fall out but, ironically, Nathan got on better with Matt than he did with either Ben or Jack. Matt always felt like my fourth son – and he's my godson too. I've always had a soft spot for him. That doesn't stop just because something terrible happens – despite the anger, and the blame and the why-why-whys?

The other day I wrote him a letter – to get a few things off my chest. Lance a few boils. Get my thoughts straightened out a bit . . .

I'm too rattled to drive so I get into the car in the darkness of the multi-storey car park and sit there for a while. I'm sobbing. Slapping the dashboard with my palms, chuntering to myself. A young woman in a four-by-four draws up beside me and starts to unfold a buggy and lift a baby out of its car seat. She glances nervously in at the window of my car. Dismisses me as a mad woman. The baby's dressed in blue so I figure it must be a boy. A son. Just you wait, I think. Just you wait.

After a while I feel much calmer so I drive home. As I put the car in the garage it comes on to snow again. There are some chaffinches in the garden eating the peanuts I put out earlier this morning. I notice the bird bath is frozen – sealed over with a cold crust – smooth as a sucked lozenge. I break the surface with the car keys and the ice crackles and splinters like creme brûlée.

Driving a silver Vauxhall Corsa down the Lower High Street at twenty-six miles an hour, Matt Fry feels the parcel of chips, warm on his legs. He grips the steering wheel with his left hand and, with his right hand, lifts hot slivers of fried potato to his lips – making his mouth a hollow 'O' and sucking in air to cool each mouthful. There is salt and ketchup on his fingers. He licks them clean as he turns left opposite WH Smith's.

The Corsa slows as he approaches a mini-roundabout, one foot on the brake, the other on the clutch. A bus passes from the right, leaving the carriageway empty behind it. Matt pauses a moment before he pulls out onto the roundabout, scooping up another mouthful of chips.

'Good chips,' says Nathan from the back seat. Matt nods in agreement. He is licking his fingers clean again.

'Shall I operate the gear stick?' Sophie says, from the seat beside him. 'I do it for my grandad when he smokes!'

'Nice one,' Matt says. He presses his left foot to the

floor and Sophie pushes the gear lever forwards into first. Matt turns the steering wheel with his left hand, flicks the indicator on with his pinky. The engine revs impatiently.

'Second gear, please,' says Matt and Sophie pulls the lever towards her. Matt eats another chip – licks grains of salt off the thumb of his right hand.

Sophie has her hand poised on the gear stick. They are off the roundabout now, heading into the one-way system, threading their way past Debenhams and Pizza Hut and BHS.

'Into third,' Matt says, accelerating slightly. Sophie leans across, pushing the gear stick towards the driver's seat. Her fingers brush his thigh.

Moments later they are passing under threads of coloured lights, hammocking across the street from lamppost to lamppost.

'Oooh! Pretty Christmas lights,' says Becci, wiping her hand on the misted glass. On each lamppost there are figures, illuminated from inside – glowing santas and snowmen with scary grins and gormless reindeers with flashing noses.

'That Father Christmas looks like a child molester,' Sophie says, giggling. 'And the snowmen look as if they're all high!' Nathan says.

They are right in the town centre now. All the shop windows are brightly lit – displaying their wares to the blank streets.

'That's the phone I'm getting for Christmas,' says Sophie as they pass a Carphone Warehouse billboard ad. She shakes her head and her rabbit ears jiggle.

'Cool!' Becci says, helping herself to a curry-smeared chip off Nathan's lap.

In front of them, traffic lights turn amber and then red. Matt slows to a halt, slips the car into neutral, holds the steering wheel lightly in his greasy fingers, pulls on the hand brake with his left hand. Suddenly a car horn toots. A yellow Renault Clio is pulling up alongside them in the outside lane.

'It's Vicky,' Becci says. Through the glass she can see four people in a car. She winds her window down to get a clearer look, identifying them one by one.

In the driving seat is Vicky, a girl from her Business Studies group who (briefly – in Year Eleven) went out with Nathan. She's dressed as an eskimo. Cute fur hood, last vestiges of black eyeliner just about visible. (Becci glances sideways at Nathan to note whether he's pleased to see her or not. He's not reacting. Becci smiles.) Beside Vicky is Dan Lucas – Elvis (one of several). In the back seat (driver's side) – Becci has to sit forward to see who it is – Justin Stoker. His costume is long since disintegrated. She remembers him at the party dressed as an escapologist – Houdini-ish in Victorian long johns and a thermal vest (his dad's apparently) all trussed up in lengths of paper party chains, with a crepe bandage over his mouth as a gag. She recalls him on the dance floor, arms pinioned to his sides and people tugging at the chains – unravelling them, uncoiling him like a spinning top. He's in his normal clothes now with only a rather smudged drawn-on curly moustache to give him away.

Next to him, with his pale queasy face pressed up to the glass like a weird fish in an aquarium, is a boy from Matt's Law group that everyone calls 'Toast'. Becci can't remember what he's really called. Steven, maybe, or Dave. Something a bit dull. 'Toast' came to the party wrapped in a grey nylon sleeping bag, saying he was an electric eel, and spent all night tripping over and annoying people. Becci last saw him (eels obviously can't hold their drink) vomiting over the fire escape. Now he looks rough.

'I think Martin's a bit pissed,' Matt says looking sideways. Martin – that was it. Martin Timewell. Matt holds up a tomato-sauce-covered chip – dangling it temptingly in Martin's direction. Martin mimes a throwing-up gesture – opening his mouth wide and splaying out his tongue.

'Gross!' says Becci.

Elvis, meanwhile, has wound his window down and is stretching out his hand towards Matt.

'I'll have it!' he says, pointing to the chip. 'Give it to me!' Matt tips his head back, like some Roman eating grapes at an orgy, and swallows the chip down in one gulp.

'Aw! Tight!' says Sophie. 'Give him one . . .'

'Feed me!' shouts Elvis from the adjacent car. He is holding out his hands in a gesture of tragic starvation. Matt laughs and winds his window down. He plucks a chip from the greasy paper on his knee and thrusts it towards the yellow Clio. But his arm isn't long enough.

'I can't reach,' Matt says, retracting his hand.

'Hang on,' Elvis shouts. He turns to Vicky and waves his hands desperately.

Laughing, she quickly reverses her car a few metres and then pulls forward again, inching up closer to the wing of the silver Corsa.

'A-da girl,' says Elvis, reaching out the gold lamé sleeve of his Teddy Boy suit towards Matt's window. The cars are now so close they are almost touching.

'Mind my wing mirror,' Matt says. He holds out the chip and Elvis takes it.

'Yeah, mind my mum's car!' says Nathan from the back seat. 'Or we'll be sending you the bill . . .'

Elvis is chomping the chip but, as he eats, he's complaining.

'Damn! I *hate* tomato sauce,' he says.

'Have one of mine,' Nathan says. 'Mine've got curry sauce on them.' Nathan stretches over Matt's shoulder, crushing Becci in the process, and thrusts his arm through the open window to put a chip into Elvis' hand.

'This one's cold!' Elvis says with mock outrage.

'God, you're fussy!' Vicky says, cuffing him across the back of his oily black wig.

'Yeah,' Nathan shouts, flopping back down in his seat. 'Ungrateful bastard!'

The lights have changed to green and behind them, a maroon Volvo is waiting to move off. In the yellow Clio Elvis is still stretching his hand melodramatically through the open window and Martin Timewell is looking nauseous. No one is watching the lights. No one is watching the road. Finally the driver of the Volvo loses patience and leans on his horn.

Becci

On the way out to the motorway we passed the bus shelter. They've replaced it now. It's dark green with smoked glass – quite swish and streamlined. The old one was red with that bubbly frosted glass that shatters into tiny cubes like grains of sugar. They left it leaning over, bent out of shape, for months. Finally Dad rang the council and shouted at someone in the highways department. He said he'd knock it down himself with a sledgehammer if they didn't come and dismantle it. It was a very un-Dad-ish thing to do – very out of character. He's normally Mr Diplomatic. Mr See-both-sides-of-the-argument. Mr Let's-sort-this-out-without-getting-cross.

I've switched channels now and we're listening to Vernon Kay on Radio One but Dad's still singing along. Mr Easily-Pleased.

There's an old lady waiting at the bus stop with a tiny white dog in a tartan coat. I wonder if she knows what happened there. The flowers are long gone, though, like the crumpled metal, they hung around an agonisingly long time. They died slowly – as flowers do – turning brown and soggy in the rain.

The Cellophane went all yellowed and tatty. I think someone nicked the rugby ball and the teddies and bits of stuff all disappeared bit by bit. But the flowers clung – rank and decomposing – on the bus-stop pole for weeks and weeks. Mum wouldn't go by. It made her too angry. Then one day – around Easter time – Dad was driving and she was in the passenger seat and he drove that way home from Waitrose without thinking. She saw the torn Cellophane and the tyre splashed loops of satin ribbon and the rotting stalks and she flipped.

She went back that night with a bin liner and a pair of scissors and she cut the whole lot down. Snipped the tape, scrumpled up the faded bows, stuffed the dead stalks – the black mouldering leaves, the cabbagey chrysanthemum heads – into the black bag and brought them all home. Shoved them in our dustbin. Someone must have seen and grassed her up because Sophie's mum rang up and screamed at her. She said she had no right to touch them. She said our family had done enough damage. She said we had no idea about the pain . . . Actually I don't know what she said, I'm just guessing. I only know the state it left Mum in. I found her sitting on the bottom step pulling tufts of wool out of the stair carpet.

Sophie should never have been in the car in the first place. Her mum – Kirsty (the one with the noodles and nail painting – the one I used to like) – was supposed to collect her from Emma's party. That was the deal. Her mum was going out for the evening, but she'd be back. Sophie was supposed to ring her about midnight. She said she'd pick her up from the party. I heard her say it – when she dropped Sophie off.

Sophie texted me to say she was arriving at the Rugby Club and I went out to the car to meet her. She was worried Matt would think she looked tarty in her fishnet tights. I thought he might but I didn't say so – obviously. Actually she looked fine. She looked pretty. Her mum on the other hand really *did* look tarty! She – Kirsty – was all dressed up – floaty top, fake tan, loads of cleavage and too much make-up. Trying too hard, in my opinion. Sophie said she'd got lucky and was going out on a date with some bloke she'd met at her dancing group. Sophie felt a bit weird about it.

'He looks dodgy,' Sophie said. We were in the loos at the Rugby Club. She was rearranging her bunny ears and touching up her lip gloss.

'I thought you hadn't met him,' I said.

'I've seen him though,' she said. 'In Tesco. Mum spotted him behind the frozen food and went all giggly.

' "That's him," she whispered at me . "The bloke I told you about from salsa!" He looked like a bodybuilder. And he was bald! At least Dad's got hair!'

Sophie's dad looks like Elvis Costello. He and Kirsty split up a few years ago and he's married again now with a new baby that Sophie calls (called) The Blob.

'What's his name?' I said, tucking my hair behind my pointy ears.

'Who?' said Sophie. 'Salsa man?' I nodded. 'Gary,' she said and she pulled a face. She turned sideways on to check that her pink fluffy tail was still attached. 'It's held on with velcro,' she said, 'so you can take it off.'

'Why would you want to take it off?' I asked.

'Because when you sit down it feels as if you're sitting on a baked potato,' she said. I smiled.

'She says he smells nice!' Sophie said suddenly.

'Yuck! Too much information,' I said.

'Exactly,' Sophie said, snapping her make-up purse shut.

Sophie rang her mum at 11.30. She said her mum sounded a bit hyper and that there was music on in the background.

'She's asking if there's any chance I can sleep over at yours?' Sophie said, putting her hand over the mouthpiece of her phone. Matt was standing behind her nuzzling his face in her hair.

'Sounds good to me,' he said, smiling like the Cheshire Cat.

'Do you need to ask your mum and dad?' Sophie said.

'Nah, they'll be fine,' I said.

Sophie put her ear to the phone.

'That's fine,' she said. 'OK. Yeah. *No*, Mum! Yeah, I love you too. Bye.' She pressed 'end call' on her handset. Matt was running his finger and thumb along one of her velvety rabbit ears.

'Sounds like she doesn't want me around,' said Sophie, looking a bit wistful. Then she smiled. 'Suits me anyway,' she said, flippantly. 'Dad's taking me Christmas shopping tomorrow – so if he picks me up from yours, at least there won't be the usual scene with Mum.'

'Just you and him?' I said.

'Yep,' said Sophie. 'No wife. No Blob.'

Matt kissed her. 'Great, then,' he said, 'let's have another dance . . .'

Kirsty

It was my first date with Gary. We went for a meal at a nice Italian place on the other side of town. I had Tagliatelle Carbonara. Sure, I was nervous. Well I would be, wouldn't I? It was my first date for nearly twenty years. We went in his car. I didn't drink that much – just a few glasses of red with the meal. I wasn't drunk – if that's what you think. But I don't like to chance it. I'd had a bit too much to drive so it worked out well for Sophie to sleep at Matt and Becci's. It was the responsible thing to do . . .

After Geof (that's Sophie's dad, my ex-husband) left me, I didn't go out for two years. I just sat around feeling sorry for myself. Getting bitter. (I went to work, obviously, but I mean I didn't go 'out' out.)

'Get a life, Mum!' Sophie used to say. It was *her* idea for me to take up the dancing. She brought me home a leaflet from the Leisure Centre. (She used to do Taekwondo there on a Thursday.)

'You should try this,' she said, 'it'll do you good! Tuesday nights.'

I didn't know what to expect. I thought it might be like *Come Dancing* – you know, all sparkly frocks and stiletto heels and people taking themselves terribly seriously. But it's not like that at all. People just wear trainers and jeans and it's a laugh. It's Cuban and the music's very upbeat and happy. Sophie was right. It *did* make me feel good. I was having fun again. That's not a crime, is it?

I'd been going to the salsa class for a couple of months when I met Gary. I was just out of the Beginners' section and into the Improvers – starting to get the hang of the moves. He'd obviously done it before – he knew what he was doing, which I liked. There aren't that many men in the group so new ones – and new ones who can dance without getting their feet in a tangle – are a welcome sight. I didn't immediately fancy him, he's not my usual type, but I thought he looked interesting – and he had a nice smile. You don't really get much chance to talk during the class because you're dancing the whole time and it's quite strenuous. (Apparently you burn as many calories as going to the gym.) Every few minutes the teacher makes you change partners so you only ever dance with one person for a short time. Also, I find I can't dance and talk at the same time so I can't have said more than half a dozen sentences to Gary in a whole month of Tuesday nights. I knew his name. I knew he was some sort of engineer. I knew he had a six-year-old son called Callum. And I knew he wasn't married to Callum's mum any more. (I'll have to admit I was pleased about that.)

Then one Tuesday we got talking – after the session, when they turn the lights down and you get the chance to dance freestyle. He bought me a drink and we sat at the side and just chatted. The following Tuesday he asked for my number and then he rang me and invited me out for dinner. It was very low key. We were taking our time. Not rushing things. Geof – my ex – made it sound like we were having a torrid affair. (Not that he can talk.) He made it sound like I'd completely abdicated my responsibilities as a mother . . .

I hardly saw Sophie for the month she was going out with Matt Fry. She was with him the whole time – joined at the hip, as they say. Occasionally she brought him round to our house but mostly she was at his. To be honest we had a few rows about that. I said she'd started using our house like a hotel – just popping back to eat and sleep there. She seemed pretty keen on him. I don't know if it would have lasted.

I didn't know the Frys that well . . . before it happened. Not that I know them much better now. But then I wouldn't want to, now. I knew *him* a bit of course – Mr Fry – from seeing him at school – at Parents' Evenings and things. He always seemed a bit pompous and self-important to me. Sophie said he was more relaxed at home. She kept going on about how funny he was. (I think she really missed *her* dad when he left – well, she was only thirteen.) Perhaps if she'd had a happier home life she wouldn't have gone round to the Frys so much. Then it wouldn't have happened, would it? (Geof didn't take *that* into consideration when he blamed me ... the way he went on you'd have thought the whole accident was *my* fault!). I did my best. And I didn't *ask* to be a single parent.

It annoyed me a bit the way Sophie went on about the Frys. What a great family they were. How close they all seemed. What nice food Matt's mum – Sally – cooked. (I cook nice food too!) I only went round to their house once, to pick her up one evening after she'd been somewhere with Matt. She (Sally) invited me in for a coffee but I was dashing so we just stood on the doorstep talking for a while. It was only small talk. Chitchat. We didn't have much in common.

I'd known Becci for a while of course. She and Sophie had been friends for a few years. Becci never made much of an impression on me though. She seemed a bit dull. Matt seemed a bit dull too, to be honest. I'm not saying he wasn't good enough for Soph or anything. But he wasn't great looking and he didn't have much to say for himself – not much charisma. Afterwards, in court, everyone went on about what a marvellous person he was – good at this, accomplished at that. Duke of Edinburgh Award, music exams, university place, high achiever – blah-di-blah. It all felt a bit inflated. A bit over-egged.

After we'd eaten (I couldn't manage a pudding but Gary had Tiramisu) we went back to my place. It must have been elevenish by then. I mentioned Sophie and the party. Gary offered to go and collect her – which was nice of him – but when she phoned she sounded pretty keen to sleep at Matt's. (I said she had to sleep in Becci's room, mind! She said his parents were non-negotiable on that one so I didn't need to worry.)

I ground some fresh coffee and Gary had a whisky. He'd been on orange juice all night because he was driving. I think *he* was nervous too. (He said he hadn't seen anyone else since he split up with Callum's mum.) The whisky made him more relaxed and he took his jacket off. I lit the scented candles Sophie had bought me at Christmas.

It must have been an hour or so later when the doorbell rang – I didn't look at the clock. Gary was in the bathroom at the time. I don't remember much about what happened after that. There was broken china on the floor the next day so I think I must have knocked something off the work surface. There were two police officers – a man and a woman. They took me and Gary to the hospital. I had to identify her.

They warned me she was a mess. The policewoman asked if Gary wanted to do the ID instead of me. I said he couldn't because he'd never seen Sophie before.

They said she was dead on arrival. They said they did everything they could.

Gary

To be honest I hardly knew Kirsty. She was just someone I saw on Tuesday nights that I quite fancied. Let's face it – when you get to my age you take every chance you get! We went out for a meal. We weren't seriously involved or anything. It was just a date – pretty casual.

One thing I can't cope with is heavy scenes. They do my head in. Claire, my son Callum's mum? She used to go ballistic sometimes and really yell at me. It was well offside. I always shut the door on her – walked out until she'd pulled herself together. You can't speak to people like that and just expect them to stick around and take it. Claire was pretty slow to get that one. It's her loss.

Kirsty went completely mental when they came to the door. I was on the loo at the time. (If it had been ten minutes earlier she might not even have answered it.) When I heard her yelling I went back downstairs pretty damn quick. The noise she was making was barely human. It was a terrible waily yowling sound. It reminded me of the noise this Alsatian dog made years ago when my dad accidentally ran it over in our road. The kitchen door was ajar. I opened it so I could see her and then I wished I hadn't. She was by the fridge, half dressed, and she was hurling stuff onto the floor. Cups, plates, cutlery. She was just throwing things onto the quarry tiles and they were smashing – bits flying everywhere.

I walked towards her and a shard of china lodged in the ball of my foot. It hurt like hell. Bled too.

'What's happened?' I shouted. 'What the fuck's happened?'

She didn't say anything. Just kept howling. I got hold of her and held her, really tight – pinned her arms against her so she couldn't do any more damage. She was thrashing about like someone having a fit. It was several minutes before she could tell me what had happened. Eventually she said, 'Sophie's dead.'

Then all of a sudden she started hitting me, pounding her fists on my chest, beating the crap out of me. (You should have seen the bruises the next day – *and* I needed two stitches in my foot.) I tell you, I almost left right then. I was thinking, 'No, lady! I don't need this!' But I'm not that callous. I helped her get dressed and find her shoes.

The police were waiting outside – 'giving us a moment of privacy' they said. If they'd seen her thumping me they might have charged her with assault!

They drove us to the hospital. It only takes ten minutes from where she lives but she must have smoked five cigarettes in the time it took us to drive there. She smoked them back to back. Chain smoked. Sucked on them like she was about to drown. I tried to hold her hand but she pulled it away.

Sophie's body was in the morgue. They asked me if I was Sophie's father. I said I was just a friend. Friend sounds better than one-night-stand, don't you think?

They asked me if I wanted to go on in as well. I said I didn't think it was appropriate. Well come on, I hadn't even met the kid! Don't get me wrong. I'm not making light of it. Nobody should have to go through that. Nobody should have to experience what Kirsty experienced. It's just – it wasn't *my* problem. I stuck around for as long as I needed to – got my foot sorted out while I was at it – and then I left.

I phoned Kirsty a few times in the weeks after that. Well, once or twice anyway. But it was never going to happen, was it – not after *that*?

David

I'm a great believer in positive thinking. I believe we can train our minds to focus on the good things – to screen off the negative. I've found – with practice (it's a bit like mental gymnastics) – that I can fence certain things off in my mind. That I can put a cordon round them and make a positive, conscious choice not to go there – not to look at them, not to dwell. There's a resulting containment – a sense of holding things safely – of avoiding toxic spillage. Most of the time this works for me. My thought-life feels quite orderly. I feel in control of where my imagination is taking me. But there are some memories that just won't stay contained. They burst out and demand to be looked at.

Stella's mangled car is one of those memories. The image of it springs out at me as we inch along, nose-to-tail, on the M5.

The traffic has slowed to a stand-still and three lanes are feeding into one. Up ahead I can see the spinning blue light of a police vehicle.

'Looks like an accident,' I say to Becci. She has her knees pulled up to her chest, her feet on the dashboard.

'Will we be late?' she says.

'Hard to say.' I switch on the wipers to clear the new falling snow off the windscreen. We're moving again, only five or ten miles an hour, but at least we're making progress. We slide nearer to the swirling blue. Suddenly an ambulance comes hurtling down the hard shoulder, siren blaring, light flashing. As we get nearer I can see what's causing the delay. There's a red Toyota, sideways-on in the inside lane, with its front wing all buckled in. Stella's car again, crashing into my thought space . . .

Matt wanted to learn to drive as soon as he was old enough. Sally and I supported him in that. I wonder about the wisdom of it now, but at the time it seemed perfectly reasonable. Sally didn't learn till she was in her thirties. I left it till I was a student and was too broke and too disorganised to have regular lessons so it took me three years and two failed tests to get my licence.

We wanted Matt to learn properly, to have good quality lessons in a concentrated block, while he was still living at home. Sally's parents offered to pay, which was a big help. Matt got his provisional licence the moment he was seventeen and we booked a block of lessons with a chap called Bob who one of my work colleagues had recommended. I took Matt out a few times before that, to Waitrose car park on Sunday afternoons, when there were no cars there –

just to get the hang of the clutch and the feel of the controls so he'd have a bit of a head start.

He did really well. Characteristically well. He was sensible – methodical – seemed to have a natural 'feel' for it. He learned quickly – much quicker than I did. After about twenty-five hours of tuition he passed his test first time. Sally's parents sent *another* cheque so we could take him out for a meal to celebrate.

We went to a pub out near Cirencester for Sunday lunch and Matt drove us all home again. I'm sure I'm not mis-remembering things – making them more rosy after the event. I felt completely safe in the car with him. We all did. He was cautious, he didn't take unnecessary risks, but he didn't dither about either. He was decisive.

After he passed his test Matt did that Pass Plus package where you have a few extra lessons to take you to a more advanced level. (It makes a big difference to the insurance premium.) We insured Sally's Nova for him to drive. He didn't use it that often, just odd climbing club trips and things. I suppose, when he started going out with Sophie he used the car a bit more often. He'd run her home in it if Sally wasn't at work. I think he quite liked having 'wheels' – well, who doesn't? – but he didn't show off behind the wheel. Not as far as I could see anyway. I don't think he drove fast to impress Sophie.

I don't think he really drove fast at all.

The papers made him out to be something of a boy racer. They suggested he was speeding for Sophie's benefit, driving recklessly because he had his girlfriend in the front seat. The *Echo* made it sound as if he was somehow trying to prove his manhood. All kinds of assumptions were made in the aftermath of the crash. That Matt was speeding excessively. That he was messing about. That he was drunk. The papers were full of lies. You wouldn't believe the number of letters I received. Not letters of support or sympathy but letters of criticism, letters of complaint, letters 'for my information'. Suddenly all traffic accidents were *my* fault. A man who I've never met (name withheld) sent me an article downloaded off the internet about restrictions and curfews that they've introduced in some parts of the USA to try to reduce road deaths caused by teenage drivers. For example in some places you can't drive after midnight if you're under 18, or you can't drive with people your own age in the car. 'Is this something we need here?' he'd scrawled across the bottom. I never replied.

When all is said and done, it was an accident. We all make mistakes. There but for the grace of God go I . . .

The traffic's flowing again now. We're past the crumpled Toyota and the cars are using all three lanes again. I look at Becci. She's closed her eyes and seems to be asleep so I retune the radio to Radio Two. Just as I reach fifty she speaks, without opening her eyes.

'Oi!' she says. 'I was listening to that!'

Becci

Matt should never have been driving that night. It wasn't his car – it wasn't *our* car. It was the Jeffersons' car – Stella's Corsa. Afterwards, the police kept asking how much Matt had been drinking. Was he drunk? Was he over the limit? Had he been unfit to drive? That was the point! Matt was driving because *Nathan* was over the limit.

Matt was never one to drink excessively. He hadn't been drinking at the party. Well, hardly, anyway. Maybe he'd had a couple of beers, but early on, hours before we were ready to go home. Matt's always been a moderate drinker. He's always said you don't need alcohol to have a good time. He was the sort of person to buy a pint and make it last all evening. Or drink Coke.

Nathan, on the other hand (typical!), was a bit inclined to go overboard.

We stayed quite late at the party – until it was going raggy round the edges and people were a bit the worse for wear. Sophie suddenly said she was cold. She looked a bit poorly too – a bit green tinged.

'Do you mind if we go?' she said. She'd just dodged out of the way of Victor Rankin who was being sick in the doorway of the gents toilet. (I thought the smell was going to make *her* be sick too.) Victor Rankin's fancy dress was looking a bit ropey. He'd come as 'Elderly Person' (beige grandad cardigan and slippers) with lines and wrinkles drawn on his face with black eyeliner and talc on his hair to make it white. (He's in the Performing Arts crowd and he's a bit theatrical.) He'd been going round all night rabbiting on about the war and waving a fake bus pass he'd made. Now – several hours and several vodkas later – his wrinkles were all smudged so he looked as if he'd just come up from a coal mine.

Elliott and a lad called Adam, who's in the climbing club with Matt, were having an eating contest. There were a load of empty take-away pizza boxes on the table. Elliott had eaten fifteen slices of pizza and was about to eat another. Adam was chomping disgustingly, tomato goo dribbling down his chin. A bloke I'd never seen before in an elephant costume was chalking up the score on the paper tablecloth.

'Ell-i-ott! Ell-i-ott!' someone shouted and he took a bow as he stuffed a slice of Margarita into his mouth.

'Gross!' said Sophie, as she went into the ladies to get her coat.

Matt – more sober than most people – was leaning

against the wall, talking to Ben, the keyboard player in his band (the one in the Everton kit). Ben was eating Jaffa Cakes from one of those tubes a mile long. I went looking for Nathan who'd given me the slip and found him (where else?) on the dance floor. He was dancing (as energetically as he had been three hours ago) with Lauren Barker, a girl I used to go to primary school with who earlier in the evening had been dressed as a sheep ('ewe') in a plastic mask and a sheepskin coat. The coat was now discarded on the back of a chair and the mask was lying in the corner all cracked and split, looking as if someone had stamped on it. Lauren Barker (I never liked her, even when she was six – she had a spiteful face) was throwing herself at Nathan, being really flirty, grabbing hold of his emu feathers, dancing really close to him with her blouse half unbuttoned. I stood at the side of the dance floor trying to get Nathan's attention. He looked as if he still had hours of partying in him but Sophie wanted to go and I didn't want to leave the party without Nathan. In fact I wanted him to act as if we were an item – which I suppose in reality, we weren't. I suddenly felt tired and bad-tempered and like I'd had too much to drink. At the end of the song Lauren Barker threw her arms round his neck and snogged him. I was sitting on a bar stool at the side of the dance floor, watching them. He wasn't exactly fighting her off. I got up and flounced out as obviously as I could.

It worked. Nathan followed me. I was putting on my coat in the corridor.

'Bex!' Nathan said. 'Don't go.'

'Sophie wants to get home,' I said, 'she's sleeping at ours.'

'Stay without her,' he said. 'I'm sure Matt can look after Sophie.' He winked at Matt but Matt was still talking to Ben about guitars and stuff.

I was feeling peeved about Lauren Barker so I said, 'Naw. I'm tired. I've had enough.' I turned away. Huffy cow!

Nathan hesitated a moment and then he said, 'I'll come too then. It's a crap party anyway.'

I turned round and looked at him to see if he was joking. He was beaming at me – the Nathan Jefferson smile – and I felt, momentarily, as if I'd won the lottery.

'Let's split?' he said, slipping his arm round my shoulder.

Matt broke away from Ben – who was stuffing a whole Jaffa Cake into his mouth – and stepped towards us. Matt was in his jeans and shirt now – the shirt he'd taken an age selecting. 'I'll ring for a taxi,' he said, pulling out his phone.

'Where's Dad's bathrobe?' I asked.

'I've got the car,' Nathan said suddenly – as if he'd just remembered he had it. 'We don't need a taxi.'

'Aren't you a bit pissed to drive?' Matt said. He was walking back onto the dance floor, looking under the chairs around the edge, tying to find his discarded costume.

'What have you lost?' Sophie said, reappearing in her coat.

'Bathrobe,' Matt said, threading his way between some tables in semi darkness.

'It's here,' Sophie said, holding up a carrier bag. 'You gave it to me ages ago. Duh!' She pulled Dad's dressing gown out of the bag and draped it round Matt's shoulders.

'ET phone home,' she said, pointing to Matt's mobile. 'Who are you phoning?'

'Taxi,' said Matt, fiddling with the handset. 'But there's no signal.'

'We don't need a taxi. I'll drive,' Nathan said.

Matt was ignoring him, walking out into the corridor, redialling the number.

A boy from my French group – Karl Zimmer man – goatee beard, shaved head, very camp – skipped past us in the corridor and said, 'Not leaving already?' His bald head was beaded with sweat and his blood-red shirt had big damp stains under the armpits.

'I just need to pee,' Nathan said, disappearing into the gents, sidestepping Victor Rankin's vomit.

'Nathan's not fit to drive,' Matt said, when he was

gone. 'He's been knocking it back all night.' Sophie was running her fingers through Matt's hair and yawning sleepily.

Nathan emerged from the toilets all smiles and kissed my left ear. 'Those pointy ears really do it for me, Becci,' he said.

'Perhaps you're really an elf,' I said.

Emma appeared from the direction of the bar. She had a piece of tinsel tied around her head and a stethoscope dangling round her neck.

'We're off,' I said. 'Matt's just sorting transport.' I gave Emma a hug and kissed her twice – once on each cheek. The tinsel scratched against my forehead.

Over her shoulder I could see Elliott stuffing another slice of pizza into his mouth. There was a cheer from the spectators and the elephant man shouted, 'Seven-teen!'

'Sorry to leave before the end of the competition,' Matt said, redialling the taxi firm for the fifth time.

'How about I text you the result?' Emma said, smiling. 'It'll end in tears,' she said.

'No, it'll end in puke,' Nathan replied.

'Fab party,' I said. 'Thanks, Emma.'

'Thanks for coming, guys,' she said.

Nathan was nuzzling my hair from behind. Oh what bliss! Emma was grinning at me with a pleased-on-my-account face, the sort of face that says 'Looks like you're well in there, girl!' I was so busy cheesing back at her that I almost stepped in something gross.

'Yuck! What's that?' I said, looking down at the floor. Between where we were standing and the fire exit there was a series of sticky red dollops of what looked like rats' intestines. The largest dollop was spilling from a Cellophane bag. Sophie looked like she might be sick after all.

'That's the remains of Karl Zimmerman's special effects,' Emma said. 'He was "Entrails"! It looks like guts but it's just dyed spaghetti. Before you got here he was running round with it in a plastic bag, thrusting it in people's faces!'

'Sorry we missed that,' Sophie said sarcastically.

'Some of the lads were lobbing it about . . . and then the bag burst,' Emma said.

'Lovely,' I said.

'No taxis for at least an hour,' said Matt, holding the phone away from his ear.

Sophie groaned and leaned melodramatically against his arm.

'Shall I go ahead and book one, anyway?' he asked.

'Whatever,' said Sophie. She was trying to sound like she wasn't bothered but it was patently fake.

'Let's just take the car,' Nathan said. 'There'll be nothing on the road at this time of night.'

I looked at Nathan. He didn't look *that* drunk. Then I looked at Matt. Sophie was looking at him with puppy eyes. I could tell she didn't want to wait an hour for a taxi.

'Why don't *I* drive?' Matt said. Sophie smiled gratefully.

'Sorted,' said Nathan, waggling his big yellow emu's bum.

'Eighteen!' shouted the elephant man, as we stepped through the swing doors.

A silver car with four people in it is heading out of town and onto the western bypass. In the back of it, a boy in a yellow emu suit feeds the last of his chips – daubed in curry sauce – to a girl in a white dress who is snuggled up against his arm. The snow is thickening again, coming down like confetti, like torn tissue. The driver flips the windscreen wipers onto double speed.

Away from the Christmas lights and the orange streetlamps the night is dark and thick. The driver clicks the headlights onto full beam. They pass farmland, fields, a herd of black-and-white cows – their white markings glowing eerily like luminous clouds.

'I'll drive to your house, Nathan,' Matt says. 'If I leave your mum's car there we can just walk round to ours.'

'Don't worry about it,' Nathan says. 'Just drop me off. Keep the car. I'll come and get it in the morning.'

'Well, it's only five minutes walk,' says Matt.

'Yeah, but it's snowing,' says Sophie.

'Whatever,' says Nathan. 'I'm easy . . .' He leans

his head against Becci's and starts beat boxing – making the sound of a drum machine with his lips. Becci can feel the vibrations of the beat resonating in her temples.

'That feels weird,' she says, smiling and pulling her head away. Just then a new song comes on the radio.

'Sophie!' Becci says. 'It's Justin!' Sophie leans forward and turns up the car stereo so that *Rock Your Body* blasts out.

'Aw, Matt,' she says with affected soppiness. 'It's our song!'

Leaning forward a second time she turns the volume knob up as high as it will go.

Mike

Stella came home from the supermarket a bit upset. I could tell from her voice when she came in the door that something was wrong. I should have stopped what I was doing but I was trying to finish off some work that I'd brought home for the weekend. I hate working Saturdays but sometimes there just aren't enough hours in the week. Stella stood in the doorway talking to me while I stared at my computer screen only half listening to her. Then I heard her bang the back door and she went outside into the garden. Through the window of my study I could see her furiously chopping off dead branches, raking leaves, moving things about.

Later – after she'd shouted at me for being, what she calls, 'emotionally unavailable' – she told me she'd bumped into Becci and David Fry. So that was it. The Fry family. I should have guessed.

Stella gives me a hard time for slipping out of touch with David. It hasn't been a deliberate policy. It just happened – over the last year. David – Matt's dad – and I go back a long way. At college we were squash partners. Then we shared a flat together. I actually introduced him to Sally. (She was my girlfriend at the time but I didn't hold that against him when he married her sixth months later!) A few years ago David and I both got ourselves mountain bikes. We used to go off cycling together on Saturdays and come back covered in mud, like a couple of kids – middle-aged boys with toys. We were doing that every other week or so up until the accident happened. We've actually done it a couple of times *since*, but it's difficult now … Saturdays are their day for visiting. To be honest though, even if there wasn't the time pressure – the lack of opportunity – there's the distance, the unspoken stuff that sits there like a big looming storm cloud.

Stella always wants people to 'deal with things'. That's her way of coping. It's also her job. She's a counsellor. She talks about strategies and emotional intelligence and 'closure'. According to Stella, it would help us with 'closure' to go with them – with David, and Sally and Becci – one Saturday. I'm not ready for that. Maybe I never will be. It's all still too raw. I feel too angry. Too guilty…

Stella talks about facing up to things. I do face up to things – I just do it differently. I keep busy at work. That's *my* survival strategy. I throw myself into business – figures and documents and deadlines and targets. Real things. Things you can measure and quantify. I leave all the slippery 'feelings' stuff to my wife.

Nathan would have been at uni by now. He'd have just been reaching the end of his first term, coming home for Christmas in a week or so. That's if he'd passed his resits – the ones he was due to take in January. He wasn't exactly busting a gut revising for them in the run-up to Christmas. I gave him a hard time about that. I gave him a hard time when he got a D in Biology the summer before as well. He wanted to go to Leeds to do Sport Science and he needed three Bs. So, in a nutshell, he'd ballsed it up. I can still picture him slumped at the kitchen table after he opened the envelope with his results in. It wasn't often Nathan got upset about anything but he was gutted. I made it worse by being hopping furious, standing over him waving the bit of paper like it was a death warrant. I called him hopeless and useless and idle. (The words come back to torment you.) It seems such a stupid thing to get worked up about now – but then lots of things seem stupid now. They seem trivial. Absurdly minor. Like I used to nag him about tidiness, about looking smart in his school uniform, polishing his shoes, making his bed. It just used to bug me that he borrowed my stuff and didn't put it back – my razor, my hand weights, my CD player, my nail clippers – I was always having to rummage around in his room for my belongings. And

I'd nag him about eating too much – swiping all the cheese from the fridge, eating all the muesli bars so there were none for other people's packed lunches, drinking all the milk last thing at night so there was none left at breakfast time. He was a greedy sod! Stella gets upset if I criticise him now – as if dying at eighteen somehow makes you a saint, as if it means that suddenly only good things can be said about you. 'Thou shalt not criticise dead people – even greedy, untidy, selfish, egotistical dead people.'

There, I'm dealing with it. I'm 'being real'!

And he was a noisy bugger too. He'd crash up the stairs if he came in late and wake us all up. Do you know what the last thing I said to him was? The last thing I *ever* said? 'Don't flush the toilet when you come in late tonight.' It's not much of a parting shot, is it – not much of a farewell message?

Nathan was going to go to Australia after his resits. He wanted to snorkel on the Great Barrier Reef. He was going to stay with my brother and his family. Instead *they* flew in from Sydney for Nathan's funeral.

I press 'save' on my keyboard and lean back in my chair. Stella has finished hacking things in the garden and is sitting on the stone bench beside the pond with her hands cupped round a steaming mug of coffee. I can see plumes of breath coming from her mouth, like smoke.

110

Upstairs, Jack is playing loud music. I just heard him bang the kitchen door. Jack does a lot of banging doors – he gets it from his mother. Jack's just coming up to his GCSEs. He's doing quite well. Moderately well. Stella says I don't praise him enough. Jack bottles things – he doesn't say much – but just the other day we had a blazing row. He said he wanted to quit the rugby team. He said he was sick of the game – didn't enjoy it any more – couldn't be bothered with training. Couldn't be arsed, basically. We were in the kitchen. I was cooking a curry. He was toasting a Pop Tart. I said he never stuck at things, that he lacked team loyalty, that he never committed to anything. Perhaps I overstated my case. He turned on me and said he bet I wished it was *him* who'd died and not Nathan. He kicked a chair over on his way out of the kitchen and broke a pane in the glass door. I yelled at him and said he could pay for new glass. More trivia again. (Some people never learn.)

Jack's joined a skater gang now and we hardly see him. He hangs around with graffiti artists. One of his mates got an ASBO for spray painting bus shelters in the town centre. Stella says spending all his time skateboarding is Jack's way of processing his grief. Bollocks!

Jack

You want me to talk about Nathan? Nathan, Nathan, fucking Nathan . . . that's all that anyone ever talks about round here. It was bad enough when he was alive. You'd have thought the sun shone out of his arse. Nathan Golden Bollocks Jefferson. My first day at secondary some daft twat of a teacher says, 'You're not much like Nathan, are you?' You could almost smell the disappointment.

When I asked if I could have Nathan's bedroom – seeing as though he isn't using it any more and it is the biggest bloody bedroom in the house – you'd have thought I'd asked if I could piss on his grave. Dad said it was an 'inconsiderate thing to say' – well sorree – and Mum took a swipe at me (verbally, not physically – she'd never do anything as non-PC as to hit me – she is Mrs Right-on Social Services after all). She said I didn't keep a small bedroom tidy so why did I think I needed a bigger one. Well, because my current one is so fucking small there's nowhere to put anything for one thing. And for another thing, Nathan isn't going to be needing his room – his walk-in cupboard, and ensuite sink and big window overlooking the garden – or any of his stuff (hi-fi stack, portable TV, purple string hammock thingy, Fender copy electric guitar) in the foreseeable future, is he? Unless he rises from the dead like Jesus (and I wouldn't put it past him).

I sometimes wonder, if it had been me that had died, would they have made this much fuss. I doubt it. I'm not Nathan after all. Not wonder boy.

Dad had a go at me for giving up rugby. I actually haven't played all season but I managed not to let them know until last Saturday. They never come and watch me anyway. (Rugby's a tosser's game. The team are all such assholes.)

Dad was frying meat and the kitchen was all smoky.

'The trouble with you is you never stick at anything,' he said, waving a knife at me.

'What about skateboarding!' I said. 'I've been doing that for five bloody years!'

'Don't swear, Jack Jefferson!' he said, chopping an onion in half with a slam of steel on wood. 'The trouble with you . . .' He started again but I interrupted him – which he hates – control-freak that he is . . .

'The trouble with me is I'm not Nathan!' I shouted.

'What's that supposed to mean?' Dad said. His eyes were smarting from the onion so he looked as if he was crying.

'You'd all have been happier if it was me, wouldn't you?'

I didn't wait to see what he said in response. I just walked out. It was the closest I've got to crying all fucking year. I kicked a chair instead.

I didn't cry at the funeral. Not bloody likely. Besides it was more like a show than a funeral. The Nathan Jefferson Show. I kept expecting him to make a guest appearance – come down some glittering staircase, or swing down on a wire like Peter Pan, wearing some ridiculous costume. Like the silly fucking show-off that he was. You might have known he'd die wearing a bloody emu costume. He couldn't die quietly, could he? Discreetly.

Even dead he dominates everything. Hogs the light. Life's changed since this time last year. It's like a long shadow's spilled over everything. And all because Nathan let that wanker Matt Fry drive Mum's car.

Becci

The traffic is moving freely again now that we've passed the motorway accident. We pass a signpost. Eleven miles to go.

I catch sight of myself in the wing mirror and instinctively put my hand over my face, over my nose. The scar is fading a little but it's still glaringly obvious.

It's the first thing people see when they meet me. I can feel their eyes glancing at it and then they look away, pretending they haven't noticed. It's about six centimetres long, running from the space between my eyebrows down the left side of my nose and onto my left cheek in a purple line – as if someone's drawn on me with marker pen. A shard of glass sliced my face like a knife. I had to have fourteen stitches. The specialist says it will fade – eventually. Like everything. Like the memories.

I shouldn't feel too sorry for myself. I got off lightly compared to the others. One major cut, a few scratches and bruises and a broken rib where the seat belt impacted. If I hadn't been wearing the seat belt I might have gone right through the windscreen.

When the car was finally still – after the spinning and the crunching and the lurching – there was a terrible silence. It was dark too. All the lights cut out. I remember reaching my hand out to touch the top of Matt's head in the seat in front of me. His hair was wet and sticky. I thought it was blood but it was actually a splat of tomato ketchup from the chips he'd been eating. Afterwards, when I was in shock and nothing seemed real, that piece of information struck me as incredibly funny.

We've always had a bit of a thing about fake blood in our family. When Matt and I were kids and we went for walks on the moors, we used to do this thing where we'd get bilberries – and squash them on our faces to look like oozing blood and gaping flesh. Once, Dad took us rock climbing and we daubed our faces with berry mush and then – when we arrived home – we ran into the kitchen moaning to scare Mum. She wasn't fooled, although the woman in the shop where we stopped for ice creams looked alarmed for a moment. It doesn't seem so funny now. In fact, it seems a bit sick . . .

It's our junction. Dad indicates left and pulls onto the slip road. As we reach the roundabout he slows and we pass IKEA and the Multiplex Cinema. Justin Timberlake comes on the radio so I instinctively turn it off. The car is too warm now. I turn down the heater.

The volume is still turned up full in the silver Vauxhall Corsa when the Band Aid song (re-released version) comes on the radio. Inside the car four people sing along, at the tops of their voices. 'It's Christ-mas time . . . . there's no need to be a-fraid . . .' The driver slows as they approach a pelican crossing on the edge of a housing estate, just beside the entrance to Waitrose car park. The lights are red. A man with a black dog is standing on the pavement waiting to cross.

'Who walks their dog at this time of night?' Matt says.

'That bloke does,' says Nathan. 'Look, he's got the night-time gear and everything.' Reflective strips, running down the sleeves of the man's jacket, catch the headlights and light up and a fluorescent band, running around the dog's collar, flashes green.

'Even his dog glows in the dark!' Becci says delightedly. 'Cool!'

The car comes to a halt. Nathan winds the window down just as the song reaches the phrase 'Put your arms around the world . . . it's Christ-mas ti-i-me!'

and their four voices blare out into the cold air. The dog-walking man is crossing from left to right. He glances at the car, looks unamused by the cheery singing, continues across the road. Nathan stretches his arm out of the car towards him and says 'Merry Christmas, sir!' in a daft cockney accent, like something from *Scrooge*. The dog looks briefly over its shoulder and wags its tail but the man – fifty something, bald, square jaw – doesn't react. The light of the pelican crossing is flashing amber. Matt is about to drive off when suddenly Nathan opens the rear door (left side) and jumps out. He runs once round the car, clockwise, singing ' "Do they know it's Christ-mas time at all?"' drums on the car roof at the end of the phrase, opens the door and climbs back in.

They drive off. The bald man is making his way along the dark pavement in the opposite direction, head down, dog straining at the leash.

'Humourless git!' says Nathan.

'Maybe he sees a singing emu every night of his life,' Becci says, laughing. 'Same old boring routine!'

The driver accelerates. They're on a forty mile an hour stretch now, open fields (white with snow) to the left, brand new tidy Lego brick houses to the right.

Matt's mobile begins to ring – his 'message received' tone – the Simpsons theme tune. He can't actually hear it above the music but he feels it vibrate in his pocket. Matt lifts his buttocks off the seat in order to pull the handset out of the front pocket of his jeans. Then he hands the phone to Sophie, who turns the radio down slightly and presses 'open'.

'Adam. Twenty-four. Love Emma,' Sophie says. 'And she's sent you a picture . . .' She clicks to see the image and then says, 'Oh God! That's vile!'

'Give us a look!' Matt says, reaching out for the phone. He glances at the screen, sees a grainy picture of Elliott in mid-vomit, bent over a pile of pizza boxes.

'Oh man!' Matt says, laughing. 'Twenty-four slices!'

'Let's see,' says Nathan from the back. He snatches the phone out of Matt's hand. Now Nathan is laughing too and Becci, leaning across him to look at the screen too, is squealing with disgust.

'What did I say?' Nathan is saying. 'It'll end in puke. Had to really!'

'Text Elliott,' Matt says. 'Tell him he's a greedy bastard!' Matt is looking over his shoulder grinning at Nathan.

'What's his number?' Nathan says.

'It's in my contacts,' says Matt. He changes down to third gear as they approach a bend.

Nathan is fumbling with the phone, pressing buttons randomly. 'How do I find your address book?'

'Give it here, you useless technophobe!' Matt says, snatching the phone back.

Now the driver has the mobile in his left hand. He holds the steering wheel with his right. With his left thumb he presses the menu button, scrolls down the list of options.

'Here, Matt. I'll do it,' Becci says, resting her hand on Matt's left shoulder. In the front passenger seat, Sophie – feeling increasingly nauseous with all the talk of vomit and pizza – is looking out of the car window. Unexpectedly she sees something – an animal of some sort – a cat? Or a fox maybe? – leap from the field wall onto the grass verge just in front of them . . .

Becci

It was the phone thing that clinched it. The police seized Matt's phone – all our phones in fact – immediately. They do something called cell-site analysis where they can track the traffic of calls and texts – and there's a chip in the phone – apparently – that has a memory of every call or text you've ever received or made. So watch it!

There was other evidence too of course. Chips (yes, more chips) for one thing. Empty wrappers on the floor of the vehicle. Ketchup splashes on the upholstery – and on Matt. Greasy fingerprints on the steering wheel. The forensic lot even swabbed Matt's finger ends.

There were the tyre marks on the road – the length and position of them – the fact that they were there at all. Initially Dad said it must have been a patch of ice. Black ice. Sounds plausible. Ice counts as 'mitigating circumstances' – ice gets you off the hook. It *was* snowing after all. It was late December. The temperature must have been close to freezing . . . But there wasn't any ice. If there'd been ice there wouldn't have been skid marks.

There were eye witnesses too. The man we annoyed at the traffic lights when Nathan was feeding chips to Dan Lucas through the window of Vicky's car – the bloke in the maroon Volvo who tooted his horn – said there was evidence of 'excessive horseplay'. He also said Matt revved the engine and swerved dangerously as he pulled away from the lights – all of which is a pack of lies. Dog-Walking Man gave evidence too. He said we were having 'a rave-up' in the car with 'disco music so loud it would wake the whole estate' and that Nathan – 'the cheeky one in the turkey costume' – appeared to be high on drugs. Drugs? That was just Nathan acting like Nathan! Everything the dog bloke said got exaggerated by the papers so that they made it sound as if we were having a drug-crazed orgy in the back of Stella's Corsa. Mum and Dad were furious. The third eye-witness was the driver of the white van. And the fourth one was me . . .

They worked out the car's speed from the length of the skid marks. Matt was probably speeding. Not drastically – 'not less than ten MPH over the legal limit' was how they put it. And that's only an estimate. But he was speeding nonetheless. Speeding, eating, mucking about and using his phone. According to the Crown Prosecution Service that made him 'dangerous' not 'careless'. The distinction – apparently – is crucial.

Sophie's mum, Kirsty, said Matt was a murderer. That's technically incorrect. 'Murder' implies an intent to kill. 'Murder' is different from 'Manslaughter' – which is different again from 'Causing Death by Dangerous Driving'. This last charge – Section 1 of the 1988 Road Traffic Act – means 'driving a motor vehicle in a way that falls well below what is expected of a competent and careful driver'. (See what a criminality expert I've become! It used to be Matt that was the legal one – he was planning to do Law at Cardiff University – A levels permitting.)

Sophie's mum was standing in our kitchen shouting when she said it (that Matt was a murderer, I mean). It must have been about a month after the accident. It was definitely before the court hearing. (I'd opened the front door to her and she'd barged past me down the hallway.) I remember Mum was hanging wet washing on the overhead pulley. Kirsty stood by the fridge freezer yelling and when Mum didn't answer her she picked up a wet towel off the table and flung it in Mum's face. Dad calmly asked her to leave. He said he'd get the police if she didn't go peacefully. She left, swearing and muttering to herself.

Kirsty lost the plot big style after Sophie died. Mum said it was guilt. Sophie's dad, Geof (Kirsty's ex – the one with the blobby baby), blamed Kirsty for the accident because she didn't collect Sophie from the party like she'd said she would. Mum said Kirsty was out of control and bitter because she felt cornered. And because bereavement makes you behave irrationally. Mum's always so nice about people – she always gives them the benefit of the doubt, thinks the best of them. All the same, Kirsty was a complete cow to Mum. In my opinion.

I didn't go to Sophie's funeral. None of us did. It was a private affair – family only. I bet it was deadly. Acrimonious. Poisonous. Geof and Kirsty can't be in the same room together without having a slanging match. His new wife's half his age and wears leopard-skin shoes and she talks like she's in an episode of *Friends*. There goes a man having a mid-life crisis!

I did go to Nathan's funeral. It was pretty mind-blowing. There were *so* many people there. Stella and Mike said they wanted it to be a celebration – a thanksgiving for their wonderful son. They'd done a big photo display of him on boards at the back of the church. Loads of piccies. Nathan as a baby, Nathan in his first rugby strip (aged three), Nathan and Matt with guitars in a talent show when they were six. (No paddling pool photos – thankfully.) Nathan in France. Nathan in a wet suit on a body board in Cornwall. Nathan in a Father Christmas costume . . .

There was even a picture of Nathan in the emu suit at Emma's party that someone had taken on their phone – big cheesy grin, yellow stockings – just hours before he died.

The service was lovely, if that's not a weird thing to say – as lovely as a funeral *can* be anyway. It was – what's the word? – 'interactive'. We all queued up to light little candles and put them in a tray of sand. Then they handed round baskets with sprigs of rosemary in them (I didn't know it was rosemary – Mum told me – apparently 'Rosemary is for remembrance' – it's something to do with *Hamlet*?) – The vicar – who was a woman (quite a groovy woman – a friend of Stella – big earrings, red lipstick) – told us to take a sprig and smell it and remember something good about Nathan. I had so many good things I could have sat there smelling it for the next three days. I took my sprig home and put it under my pillow. I could still smell it weeks afterwards.

During the service – just after they'd played this bizarre thrash-metal track – Stella read a poem that she'd written herself – about Nathan's noisy feet. It's funny how you can laugh and cry at the same time. I was sitting behind a load of guys from the rugby team and all their backs were shaking. Reading a poem at your own son's funeral? I just can't imagine doing that. Stella's incredible. At the funeral she had this kind of glow – despite everything that had happened. Maybe it was shock. Maybe it was numbness, or hysteria. Whatever it was, she was really lovely to us. (I still had my stitches in and panda-black eyes.) The Jeffersons asked us to sit on the front row of the church with them – as if we were family – but Mum said she couldn't face it. So we sat quite near the back. Dad held my hand the whole way through. He held my hand with his left hand and Mum's with his right.

The silver Vauxhall Corsa is travelling at 46mph, nearing a right-hand bend on Broadfarm Road, when a fox runs into its path. The driver is still fiddling with his phone – straining to see the postage-stamp-sized screen. He has located Elliott's name in his list of contacts. He presses 'select', glancing at the keypad. He is only half-concentrating on the road. He is singing along to the Band Aid song . . .

The fox – scrawny and long and the size of a small spaniel – leaps from the grass verge onto the carriageway, making a headlong kamikaze dash for the other side of the road.

Sophie, hugging the blue checked bathrobe round her shoulders, shouts,

'MIND OUT!'

As she shouts, she instinctively flings her hand out to the side, slapping Matt in the chest.

In the driving seat Matt reacts instantly. He looks up from the phone, startled.

Becci and Nathan, leaning through the gap between the two front seats to see Matt's mobile, look up to catch the fox's eyes gleaming through the falling snow like two amber beads.

The fox, pausing momentarily to stand statue-like, as if petrified by the headlights' glare, is directly in the way of the speeding car. Matt – still steering one-handed, cradling his mobile in his left palm – swerves right, swinging out onto the right-hand side of the road. He misses the fox. Nathan, glancing out of the rear window, seeing nothing but inky blackness, says, 'How many points for a fox?' He is laughing. He shouts loud above the noise of the radio . . .

But immediately – even as Nathan speaks – they are into the bend, white chevrons gleaming on the warning sign ahead. Here, the road veers sharply to the right, thick hedges on the curve concealing the road beyond. The driver knows this road well. They are under five minutes from his house. He knows that beyond the bend is a straight stretch where hedges give way to pavement and fields give way to houses – a neat cul-de-sac with mock Tudor houses, curved lawns, low-maintenance gardens with shrubs and patches of gravel. The driver knows that after the bend on the left-hand side there is a long verge, streetlamps, iron safety railings, a bus stop. He has waited at this bus stop, often, to catch the number 503 to his bass guitar lesson. The bus shelter is a metal one, red, rectangular, with glass sides. It usually smells of urine and cigarette ends.

Suddenly – too late – Matt sees the lights of an oncoming vehicle, rounding the bend, travelling in the opposite direction. The Corsa is still on the wrong side of the road, well over the white line markings and into the right-hand carriageway. A white van is coming straight towards it.

'SHIT!'

Immediately Matt drops his phone. It lands in the well below the hand brake. He grabs the steering wheel with both hands and slams it over to the left. But the speed he is travelling at and the severity of the turn sends the car into an anti-clockwise skid so that the back end of the Corsa spins, waltzer-like, across the white line into the path of the van. Becci, screaming in the back seat, is flung against the right-hand passenger door, with Nathan – thirteen stone with no seat belt to restrain him – thrust against her. Nathan's weight is crushing her. She can barely breathe. They are still on the wrong side of the white line.

'FUCK!'

Now Matt flips the wheel right to try and counter the skid. Becci's head jerks from side to side like a rag doll as immediately he steers left again, slamming the wheel hard on. Through the side window Becci can see the blazing lights of the van directly in front of her, like two demonic eyes. She feels for the handle on the inside of her door and pushes against it with all her strength, locking her arms to force herself away from the side of the car, arching her back against the bulk of Nathan.

In the passenger seat at the front, Sophie's eyes are wide with fear. She pulls her knees up to her chest and covers her eyes with her arms, folding herself into a ball – foetal, vulnerable, instinctively self-protective.

The driver of the white van throws his steering wheel left, lurches towards the inside curve of the bend, narrowly misses a tree, skids ominously. Matt has his steering locked on full, struggling to pull the Corsa far enough over to get out of the van's pathway. He doesn't think he can make it. They are going to hit. They are going to collide . . . He accelerates to try and give himself more time. The Corsa and the white van are almost on top of each other. Matt can see the illuminated face of the other driver – angry, incredulous eyes, mouth wide, shouting abuse. In a futile gesture, Matt leans left, as if the redistribution of his weight will somehow tilt the car out of the line of fire, like steering a bike. Jamming his foot on the brake, he waits for the moment of impact . . .

Somehow – God knows how – the vehicles miss each other. Almost. They just touch, skimming, right wing against right wing, like a brush of steely fingertips. Only the van's wing mirror is smashed. Becci hears it crunch as it flies off.

'JESUS!'

But now the silver car is careering left, ploughing towards trees on the bend, still travelling at considerable speed. Matt slams the wheel right to try and take the corner. As he steers right, the back end of the car whips left, flicking like a giant pinball lever. Nathan is flung along the back seat away from Becci. He cracks his head on the panel beside the rear left-side door and Becci hears him yell with pain.

The music inside the car goes on blaring. Now everything seems to go into nightmarish slow motion . . .

The Vauxhall Corsa, slung first left and then right in a crazy slalom, is spinning clockwise so wildly that the front of the car swings into the right-hand lane, diagonally straddling the white line. Matt tries to steer out of the skid but he has lost control now. He attempts to brake but the car only skids more violently . . . flying off the bend, ricocheting sideways down the straight, towards the pavement, towards the railings . . .

There is a screeching sound, the smell of burning rubber. Now Nathan is pressed up against the left side of the car and Becci is thrown against *him* – as in some sick fairground ride – leaning uncontrollably, heavy as stone.

Sophie is screaming hysterically. The motion of the car has swung her round so that she faces the driver, her left shoulder pressing against the passenger window. She reaches out and grabs at Matt's arm to try and pull herself away from the side of the car, clutching at the sleeves of his shirt, now damp with sweat.

'PUT THE FUCKING BRAKES ON!'

Matt has his foot pressed to the floor, braking. He doesn't know which way to steer – left to pull the vehicle out of the skid, or right to swing it away from the metal railings. The car, seemingly oblivious – like a crazed beast with a mind of its own – is hurtling sideways. Matt, frozen with panic, braces himself, locking his arms at the elbows, gripping the steering wheel until his knuckles are white, desperately forcing both his feet to the floor. But the car will not be stopped. It is intent on its course, like a bolting horse, like a runaway train. It is heading for the bus stop, broadside on, crashing onwards, as if flung from some enormous catapult. It mounts the pavement, flips up slightly as it impacts the kerb.

Then, with a sickening bang it slams into the bus shelter, crumpling like a polystyrene cup.

Becci

I feel guilty about everything. Guilty that I came out alive. Guilty that they died and I didn't. Guilty that I made Nathan leave the party before he wanted to. Guilty that I didn't stop Matt from driving. Guilty that I grassed Matt up . . .

My evidence was crucial. I was the only surviving witness. I told the truth – of course. But I didn't tell the whole truth – not at first. I missed bits out. I glossed over things. I was vague about details that I thought might be incriminating. Like the phone. But they find out anyway. They bombard you with facts, with questions, with cross-examinations . . .

I tried to make out that Matt didn't touch the mobile – that he heard the message signal but didn't open it. But they can tell. They have records. They knew the exact time the picture message was opened. They knew it was minutes – seconds – before the crash. I tried to cover for him – to say it was me who opened the message from Emma, me who started sending a reply to Elliott. But they didn't believe me. Matt's fingerprints were on the handset. There was chip grease on the keypad. My fingers were fat free.

And the phone was down beside Matt's seat.

He was to blame. *He* was the guilty one. Is that why I feel so bad? Am I trying to take some of the blame off Matt? Trying to share it out a bit? Trying to atone for something?

Stella says it's normal for people to feel guilty when they've had a narrow escape from something. She says people feel like that when they survive train crashes, or earthquakes, or terrorist attacks. It's part of the relief mechanism – the flip side of gratitude. Thank God it wasn't me . . . But why shouldn't it have been me?

Stella's a good listener. That's her job. She listens to people. I used to go round to the Jeffersons' house and talk to her about all sorts of things. Before. She's easier to talk to than Mum or Dad. She gives you the sense that nothing you say will shock her. I'd sit at her kitchen table and help her chop things – onions, carrots, slivers of red pepper – and I'd tell her secrets. Ask her advice about stuff. The only thing I didn't talk to her about was how I felt about Nathan. But I think she knew that anyway. Intuited it.

Even afterwards I'd go and visit her. In the early days. Before the case came to court. When my face was still healing. But it was too weird. There was a big hole in the house where Nathan should have been . . .

* * *

Traffic has slowed again on the motorway. No accident this time – as far as we can see – just too many cars. Saturday lunchtime, four weeks before Christmas . . . We draw up alongside a shiny red transporter lorry – laden with eight new cars – all blue, all identical, all faceless and blank, without number plates. I watch the transporter's wheels turn slowly and its tyres spray up jets of rain from the road surface, like lazy fountains. I remember how Matt had a toy transporter like this one when we were little and how I used to like pressing the button to make the top deck fold down flat. (I remember too that I cried when he swapped it with Gavin Crabtree for a Power Ranger bendy toy.)

I think of Stella again – remembering her perfume as she hugged me in the doorway of Waitrose. One day – when I was at their house after the accident (maybe it was even the last time I was there . . .) – I had a conversation with her about forgiveness. She was making bread at the time. The kitchen smelt all warm and yeasty. Stella let me knead the dough. Slam it down on the kitchen bench. Pound it and pummel it. Beat the living daylights out of it. 'It's good therapy,' she said.

She asked if I was angry. I said I was but I didn't know why. Stella said I had to forgive myself. She said we *all* had to forgive ourselves – and each other. I had to forgive Sophie for making a fuss about waiting for a taxi – for making Matt feel he had to get her home from the party as soon as possible – for making him drive against his better judgement. I had to forgive Kirsty for screeching and making Mum cry. I had to forgive Nathan for drinking too much, for arsing about in the car, for not wearing his seat belt. And I had to forgive Matt – for making a mistake.

Stella said *she* had to forgive Matt too – that being bitter wouldn't bring Nathan back. That it would only damage *her*. I remember she said that getting to a place where you can forgive someone was a journey, sometimes a long journey. I wonder if she's got there yet. I wonder if she's forgiven him. I wonder if you ever can when someone does something so terrible. So permanent.

We drive through an industrial estate, past faceless warehouses, to a mini-roundabout. Dad indicates right and we pull into the car park. I always hate this bit – the first sight of it. High flat walls. Beige. Pebbledashed. Absurdly high. Higher than any walls I've ever seen anywhere else. Ever. And the curls of wire along the top. Razor wire. As if he was Hannibal Lecter.

I pick up the carrier bag of sweets, slip my feet back into my shoes, fasten my scarf around my neck, look at myself in the vanity mirror on the sun flap. We get out of the car and walk silently towards the visitors' bungalow.

'VO?' says a security guard in a day-glo green jacket. Dad reaches into his inside pocket and pulls out a piece of paper – our visiting order. Our VO. We present our ID – Dad has his passport and mine in the silky inside folds of his jacket. The guard looks up and scrutinises us – checking that our faces fit the photos they took on our first visit. No mistaking me. Distinctive facial scarring. He nods. We are bonafide visitors. Not terrorists. Not jail breakers. Not cocaine smugglers. I read the notices about the things I can't do. According to the 1952 Prison Act I can't help Matt to escape (there's a surprise), can't convey alcohol or tobacco to him (it doesn't mention satsumas), can't convey letters 'or other articles' out of the jail for him – maximum penalty £1000. I think – as I always think – that a thousand pounds seems a small price to pay for helping your brother escape.

I think of *The Shawshank Redemption* – Matt's favourite film, ironically enough – and wonder, if I was to bring him a rock hammer, would he tunnel his way out? (Apparently he has a picture of Cameron Diaz on his wall – that someone swapped him for three bottles of Robinsons barley squash and a packet of Rizlas. He could use it to hide the hole – like Andy Dufresne . . .) I'd never get the rock hammer in though. I read the vast list of prohibited articles: no aerosols, no umbrellas, no alcohol, no scissors, no metal combs, no knives, no firearms, no drugs, no tools, no Blu-Tack or chewing gum (that one always puzzles me), no mobile phones. I hand over my phone and they give me a number tag, like a cloakroom ticket. Dad gives them his pocket knife and a stick of Wrigley's spearmint that he finds in his trouser pocket.

I give the guard my Waitrose bag and he takes out each item, feeling it, examining it. One by one he hands the objects to his colleague, who puts them through a scanner, presses a button, watches a screen. What do they suspect? That I've hidden a metal file inside the Crunchie bar? That there are razor blades concealed in the satsumas? Sachets of heroin in with the Maltesers? They give me a grudging nod, hand the carrier bag back to me. It is one p.m. Our allocated time slot is one-thirty p.m. Dad gets a scummy coffee from the vending machine and we sit down on orange plastic chairs.

A white van lurches off the bend on Broadfarm Road. It slows to a halt and pulls up on the grass verge. The driver turns off the engine. As the van shudders into silence he hears an appalling bang behind him. He pauses for a minute to catch his breath, grips the steering wheel with both hands – arms straight out in front of him – and bows his head as if praying. Grateful. Horrified.

After a moment he sits up, switches off his headlights, takes the key out of the ignition, switches on his hazard warning lights. He notices a sharp pain in the back of his neck, and reaches up to rub it. Sorely, wincing as he does, he reaches across the empty passenger seat and opens up the glove compartment. He takes out his mobile phone. Switching it on, he dials '999'.

When a voice asks him which of the emergency services he requires he says, 'All three . . . probably. There's been an accident . . .' His voice is husky and hoarse. He coughs to clear his throat, continues to answer the calm questions, reaches for the *A-Z* map on the dashboard to describe exactly where he is. He is not from round here. He is two hundred miles from home . . .

In the glove compartment is a slightly crushed packet of Marlboro Lights. He hasn't smoked for six months. These are his brother's. He fumbles with the dented red cardboard, flips open the lid, pulls out a cigarette. Holding it between shaking fingers he gropes for a lighter, finds one in the dip behind the gear lever, flicks it into life, puts the cigarette in his mouth. Unsteadily, he lights the tip, sees the flame from the lighter flash in front of him, its brightness reflected in the blank windscreen. He sucks hard, as if the cigarette will save him, stop him from drowning.

After a few desperate puffs he grabs his coat off the back seat and opens the door. He steps out onto the verge, closes the door behind him, looks at the damage done by the glancing blow. There isn't much to see. Running his hand along the wing he can feel a long scratch in the paintwork, and the side mirror has snapped right off. But he knows he has got off lightly. The van driver notices that his knees are shaking, light tremors running all through him. He feels sick, too – not at the damage ('It's only a heap of metal when all's said and done, it'll mend. A couple of hundred pounds max and anyway, the other guy's insurance will pay . . .') but more at the thought of what might have happened . . .

Suddenly he hears a girl's voice screaming. It sounds some distance off but it slices through the freezing night air like an arrow. Gripping the cigarette between his lips, the van driver thrusts both arms into the sleeves of his coat and sets off walking, back the way he has come.

There is no moon. The sky is thick and black. He can only just make things out. He sees the hedge and the tree he narrowly missed. He sees the curve of the road, the beginning of the pavement, the dark stripes of the safety railings. He crosses the road onto the opposite side. Now, catching the light spill from a nearby streetlamp, he can see the outline of the silver Corsa, nose inwards to the pavement, still and lifeless as a rock, all its lights extinguished. Speeding up, the van driver walks towards the car – walks towards the screaming. As he gets closer he can make out a mosaic of broken glass on the road, the twisted shapes of aluminium and steel, folded chaotically together, and strange pools of something – dark and spreading – seeping onto the wet tarmac like creeping shadows. Instinctively, fearing petrol spillage, the driver stops and extinguishes his cigarette under his shoe. As he looks down at the road and rotates the ball of his toe to grind out the cigarette's glow, he feels a stab of pain below his right ear, clutches at it with the palm of his hand . . .

Then he sees her. Staggering from the wreckage of

the car. Coming towards him. A girl in a long white dress. Ghostlike. Blood-spattered. Crimson rivers streaming from her face. Screaming.

Mike

Stella didn't see Nathan until the next day. I had to talk her out of it – me and two police officers together – like King Cnut pushing back the tide. She wanted to see him there and then. She wanted to touch him and hold him. 'We can't clean up the body straight away because we'll be destroying vital evidence,' the policewoman explained. 'I think your wife will find it very distressing.'

What about me? Wouldn't I find it distressing too?

I had to go to the mortuary to identify him. They'd taken him straight there from the crash. No ambulance. No A and E. No point. He was dead already.

'Life extinct' was how they put it. Straight into a body bag.

There was a label on his wrist like the ones they tag you with when you go into hospital. Only this one was impersonal – as if Nathan was a piece of luggage or something. It just said, 'Rear nearside passenger. White. Male. Vehicle One.' I saw Nathan's foot first, as they folded back the sheet of plastic that was covering him. I recognised his trainers, though they were sliced and mangled and soaked in blood. His right leg still had shreds of the yellow stocking he was wearing as part of that flipping emu costume but his left leg was like a piece of meat – crushed beyond recognition.

When I saw his face I was violently sick. They must have been expecting it. A bloke in green overalls was standing by with a bucket.

Apparently Nathan's head went right through the window. He wasn't wearing his seat belt, the stupid bugger. The rest of him – fat yellow emu body and all – got crushed as the wall of the bus shelter burst into the car. 'Major intrusion', the report said. It took them nearly an hour to cut him out. He had chronic organ damage, and a broken neck (snapped third vertebra – the same one that breaks when they hang you). They said he'd have been dead in seconds. They said he'd have lost consciousness immediately. No pain.

My mind tries to reconstruct his last moments endlessly – like a loop tape video you can't switch off. I wonder what he said, what he did, what he thought. Becci Fry said, in the course of giving her evidence at the trial, that moments before the crash Nathan said something jokey and flippant about a fox. She said he was laughing as the car spun out of control. How bloody typical is that?

But what did he say after that, as the car careered towards the bus stop? He must have said something? Must have shouted or screamed or tried to stop it from happening. Did he yell at Matt? Matt didn't say. In fact, Matt's account was flaming unsatisfactory. Too cloudy. Too vague. Like muddy water. He kept saying he couldn't remember things.

So I can only wonder. What went through Nathan's head in those last moments? What was he most aware of as the car hit the bus shelter? Did he feel terror? Did he know his life was over? And most importantly of all, did he feel loved?

David

Moulin Rouge – that was the movie we'd been watching. It was good outrageous escapist nonsense. I was singing *The Show Must Go On* – loudly and out of tune – as we went upstairs to bed and Sally was giggling. I was behind her, pushing her up the steps with my hands at the base of her back because she said she was too tired to walk. She'd been working a lot of extra shifts in the run-up to Christmas and she was shattered. Plus we'd drunk a whole bottle of Merlot between us. She got into bed without taking her clothes off and was out for the count the moment her head hit the pillow. I remember I was saying something about Nicole Kidman not looking very ill considering she was dying of TB and Sally didn't answer . . .

Sally didn't hear the phone. She's a good sleeper. Or at least, she used to be. I was dozing – in that twilight zone between oblivion and reality – being sung to sleep by Ewan Macgregor on a starlit rooftop above Paris. I picked up on the third ring. In my experience – limited as it is – policemen have unmistakable telephone voices. It's something about the grave, flat, unemotional tone they adopt, and the language they use – words like 'incident' and 'vehicle' and 'investigations'. Even before he said the word 'accident' my head was running imaginary scenes of Matt or Becci – or both of them – injured. Or worse . . .

The policeman said there'd been a collision involving a vehicle in which Matthew and Rebecca were travelling. 'Which vehicle?' A silver Vauxhall Corsa, S reg. 'Why were Matt and Becci in a silver Corsa? Whose car was it? Was it a taxi?' My brain couldn't make sense of what he was saying. (Stella hadn't had that car long so I didn't recognise the description or the registration number. Anyway, if Sally and I ever went out anywhere with the Jeffersons we always went in Mike's car – which is an Audi.) The police officer mentioned Nathan's name – and Stella's. So it was Stella's car – 'Mrs Jefferson's'. He said they were detaining the driver for questioning. Who was the driver? Stella? Nathan? No, Matthew. Matthew Fry. It took me a moment for the penny to drop. The policeman was talking about Matt. *Matt* was the driver? But why? How? Why was Matt driving Stella's car? Surely he wasn't insured to drive it? So where was Nathan? It didn't make sense.

And all I wanted to know was 'Were they hurt?' 'Are they OK?' He said Becci (Rebecca) had been taken to A and E with 'minor facial injuries' and that

Matthew had a small amount of bruising. (Great floodtides of relief.)

'And others?'

'There were two fatalities.'

'My God!'

I walked round to Broadfarm Road – it's only half a mile from our house – worried that I might be over the limit with the amount of wine I'd drunk. I was worried that I might have an accident too, especially given the agitated state I was in. The cold air met me as I opened the front door, waking me up, hauling me back to reality. I walked along pavements covered in melting snow, slushy and wet, wondering what the hell I was going to find. (I'd decided to leave Sally sleeping, which it turned out, was a mistake. She was mad that I hadn't woken her. She said it made her feel patronised, peripheral. I wasn't thinking straight. It felt as if I was trapped inside a bad dream.)

They'd put cones around the car and the bus shelter and strips of that red and white plastic tape. Half the carriageway was closed and a traffic cop was standing in the road, waving cars past on the other side. Not that there was much traffic at that time of night. There was a lot of activity at the scene. There was a fire engine and firefighters were cutting someone out of the twisted wreckage. Crash investigators were examining the skid marks, shining lights onto the surface of the road, measuring things with tapes and clipboards. There was no sign of an ambulance but two police cars were pulled up on the grass verge, blue lights flashing. I looked into the back of one of them and saw a man with tattooed arms and a neck brace.

'Can I help you?' a policewoman said, winding the window down.

'I'm David Fry,' I said. 'Matthew's father.'

'He's in the other car,' she said, pointing.

Matt looked terrible. Fat lip, pale face, sunken eyes. But worse than that, he looked haunted. Someone had put a blanket round his shoulders but he was visibly shaking, twitching like a fish on a line. When he saw me he started to cry. I got into the back seat of the car beside him. Gingerly, I put my arm around him, feeling self-conscious, feeling as if I was crossing some invisible line. We're not a very touchy family. When, I wondered, had I last hugged him? When he was ten maybe? Or eleven? Not recently, that was certain. Not since he'd got as tall as me. Taller.

When Matt felt my arm, he leant against me and started to sob. 'I'm sorry, Dad,' he said. 'I'm sorry . . . I'm so sorry . . .'

The coffee is diabolical. Every time I mean to bring a flask of drinkable stuff. Except that they probably wouldn't let me through with it, in case I was planning to use it as a lethal weapon. Or in case it was full of whisky. Or vodka. Or Carlsberg Special Brew. I am the father of a criminal after all. Guilty by association.

They call out our name and we walk across the car park towards the entrance point. More guards. More ID checks. More cross-questioning. We step through the automatic doors. Becci smiles at me, reassuringly. Putting on a brave face. She's a good girl . . .

I empty the contents of my pockets into a plastic dish – car keys, handkerchief, some loose change, a Biro – and they slide them onto a conveyor belt, through a scanner. It's like airport security without the prospect of a holiday in the sun. I walk through the body scanner. Nothing bleeps. No concealed shotgun. (Surprise, surprise.) A bloke frisks me, like a nightclub bouncer, scudding his hand across my chest, down the arms of my jacket. I feel the usual mounting sense of outrage, of violated dignity. I'm a Deputy Head Teacher, I'm a member of the Rotary Club, I'm forty-five years old, I've been unerringly faithful to my wife for twenty-two years, I go to church at least four times a year (and used to go much more). I am good. I am respectable. But every time I go through this – every time they search me, every time I walk through this scanner – I feel as if I'm hiding something. I feel deep, lurking, inexplicable shame.

We walk into the tunnel and stand, feet apart, on the red painted footprints while a sniffer dog – a long-haired German Shepherd thing (called Snoopy, apparently) – comes by us and pokes my legs with its wet nose. Its nostrils are all aquiver. Even the dog thinks I'm dodgy.

We go up the stairs, through the sliding doors, and into the Visiting Room. A guard escorts us to the computer. He asks me my name, checks the paperwork, tells me to put my thumb on the scanning device so he can match my fingerprints to his data base. A mug shot photo of me flashes up on the screen.

'Thank you, Mr Fry,' he says cheerily. 'Have a nice visit!'

He shows us to our allotted seats. The seats are blue and red plastic, bolted to the floor, arranged – four of them together – around a small round plastic table like a Wimpy bar. I sit down and Becci sits opposite me.

'Shame Mum didn't come,' she says. I nod. I think of Sally, drifting round the house in her dressing gown. Sally hates coming here even more than I do. She says it makes her feel dirty. As though she needs to take a bath afterwards.

We wait for Matt to arrive. I look around at the other inmates. I look at their families, their mothers, their brothers, their girlfriends. They're all just kids.

The Visiting Room is big with several rows of tables and chairs – all in little groups of four. Most of them are full. There's a hubbub of noise. At the table next to ours a spotty-looking girl younger than Becci is waiting with a crying baby on her knee. I notice Becci watching her out of the corner of her eye, uneasy. I think – as I often do – that, apart from the guards and the slightly threatening, edgy atmosphere, it's a bit like being in a school canteen or a doctor's surgery waiting room. It's not unpleasant. They've made an effort with the décor. The walls are a cheery blue. There are flowery curtains – blue and yellow – and one of those wallpaper borders with criss-crossing yellow roses on it. All over the walls there are bright posters – motivational, educational, full of positive messages. Healthy eating, quitting smoking, good parenting, safe sex. But for all it looks like a school or a well-run health centre there's no mistaking it's a prison. Through the window I can see the barbed wire and the automatic sliding steel gates – like Jurassic Park.

'Do you think he'll mind that I've got his jumper on?' Becci says.

'I doubt it,' I answer.

Stella

I love gardening. There's something wonderfully therapeutic about tending things that grow – pruning, and weeding and raking and new planting.

Everything in the garden looks very dead at the moment. Dead and wintry. We've had a lot of wind lately so there are leaves and branches everywhere and it's messy and chaotic.

So after I've unpacked the shopping, I put on my wellies and a pair of suede gloves and do some tidying – moving debris onto the bonfire pile down beside the apple tree and raking up barrowloads of soggy leaves. In the soil, underneath where the carpet of rotting leaves has been, I notice the first fingertips of spring bulbs, poking through bravely – luminous green and absurdly bright.

When I've finished (or rather stopped, because my back is aching) I sit by the stone bird bath and drink a cup of coffee. Mike comes out and joins me there. He brings me a chocolate biscuit on my favourite plate. He means it as a gesture of reconciliation so I apologise to him for flouncing out of his study and banging things. Mike has said on occasions that he feels as if I use him as my 'lightning conductor' – that I unleash on *him* rage that's really directed at other people and things. He's right of course. That's what in psycho-babble terms we called 'projection'. We get angry about something vague and intangible (loss, for example) and so we pin that sense of anger on something else that annoys us – something that we can more easily identify. Thus – I feel frustrated and helpless that Becci and Sally won't talk to me so I 'earth' that on Mike and the fact that he only half-listens to me. Bingo! Which isn't to say that Mike *can't* be deeply annoying at times – but then . . . can't we all?

Mike sips coffee from a Homer Simpson mug and apologises that he didn't switch off his computer and have a proper conversation when I came in from the supermarket. He takes hold of my hand – still clad in its gnarly suede gardening glove – and we sit side by side on the icy cold bench, watching a blue tit clinging upside down on the peanut feeder.

'*I'd* like to be able to hang upside down by my feet,' Mike says with a grin. I smile but I find I am still brooding about Matt and his family.

'Do you think I should go and see Sally?' I say, distractedly.

Mike slips off the glove, exposing my bare hand, and runs his thumb along the tops of my fingers. 'I think you should go, if you want to,' he says. Very open-ended. Very non-directive. Leaving me to make up my own mind – which is fair enough.

I slide my hand away and stand up. 'My bum is freezing,' I say, putting the last of my chocolate biscuit into my mouth. 'If I sit here much longer it will drop off!'

'What an interesting thought,' Mike says, raising his eyebrows. 'I could sell it on e-bay! Bottom – very good condition – one careful lady owner!' He tips the dregs of his coffee onto the gravel.

I make pizza for lunch. I mix dough and knead it and put it in a bowl by the stove to rise. When it's all warm and springy I tear off chunks and roll out each piece into a flat, creamy disc. Then I put the circles of dough onto oily baking trays and leave them to rise a bit more. The kitchen smells delicious and yeasty.

Jack likes choosing pizza toppings (olive and pepperoni is his current favourite) so I go upstairs to see if he wants to help me. He is sitting at the computer in his bedroom listening to music. The door is partially open but I knock all the same.

'Yep,' he says abruptly. I go in, handing him the plastic canister I've bought at 'X-Treme' as a peace offering.

'Bearings,' I say. 'Lucky Sevens, Titanium – did I get the right thing?'

He takes them from me, looks at them, sets them

down on his computer workstation, adjacent to the keyboard.

'Cheers,' he says. I take that as a yes. It's not quite a 'thank you' but it's an acknowledgement of sorts. Better than a grunt.

I sit down on his bed, choosing not to notice that it is unmade and covered in dirty clothes. I can see the computer monitor from where I sit. On the screen Jack is watching grainy video footage of skateboarders. I watch closely, recognising a flight of steps outside the town hall, a metal bench in the park beside the library, a wall near Waitrose car park. One of the skaters hurtling and leaping his way through this urban landscape is obviously Jack though I can't tell which one since they are all wearing hoodies and moving like greased lightning.

'Is this you?' I say, taking an interest.

'Yep,' Jack says.

'How did you film it?' I ask.

'Joel's video camera,' he says. I'm not sure who Joel is (is he the one with black greasy hair, or the tall one with blackheads, or the one who wears a brown woolly hat pulled right down over his eyes?) but I don't say so. I watch in silence, impressed at their skill, disconcerted by how dangerous it all looks. They are leaping, twisting, hurtling – defying gravity.

'That's me,' Jack says suddenly, pointing at the screen. He pauses the film, rewinds it, plays that section again. 'Three sixty flip,' he says, looking pleased with himself.

I watch the next trick. That is Jack too. I can tell, now that my eyes are tuned in – I recognise his jeans and his shoes, and the red underside of his board that I walk past every day in the porch.

'What's that move called?' I ask – hoping he won't think I am faking keenness, hoping he won't fly off the handle and call me 'patronising'. He doesn't.

'Five-o grind,' Jack says. I get up off the bed and go and stand behind his chair, so that I'm closer to the screen.

'This bit's great,' he says. He isn't even trying to hide his enthusiasm, now. 'Look at this sal flip Joel does under the bridge . . .' I look at the screen and see a stone bridge I don't recognise.

'Where's that?' I say.

'Near the station.' Jack rewinds and plays the trick again, freeze-framing it with Joel suspended miraculously several feet above the ground. I realise now that Joel is the one in the woolly hat. I wonder how he can possibly see where he's going, but again I button my lip.

I watch the video run – one amazing stunt after another – until the screen turns blue.

'That's cool,' I say. I wonder, as I say it, if 'cool' is still an OK thing to say.

Jack clicks the mouse and his desktop wallpaper

comes up on screen – a graffiti image with unreadable lettering in loud, psychedelic colours. Rocking back in his chair Jack picks up the tube of bearings, opens the lid, tips them out onto his hand.

'How much do I owe you for these?' he says, glancing over his shoulder at me.

I had intended to make him pay – that was the understanding when I said I'd get them – but in a moment of spontaneous generosity I say, 'Don't worry about it. My treat.'

Jack smiles, letting his mask slip for an instant. He looks, just briefly, like my little boy again – all open and shiny-faced. I rest my hand momentarily on his shoulder and say something I haven't said in a while.

'I love you, Jack Jefferson.'

There is a pause. Jack doesn't answer, doesn't look round. But in the glass face of the monitor I can see his reflection as he blinks back tears.

'I'm making pizza,' I say. 'Do you want to help fix the toppings?'

After lunch I drive to the Frys' house. Because Becci only mentioned David being in the car – and not Sally – I bank on the likely scenario that they have gone off without her and that I'll therefore find Sally at home by herself. I pull up on their drive beside Sally's Nova and ring the doorbell. Sally opens the door, just as I'd hoped. She is dressed (I had half expected to find her in pyjamas) and has on a pair of yellow rubber gloves, which are dripping soap suds onto the wooden floor.

'Oh,' she says. For a moment I think she is going to close the door in my face. But she doesn't.

'Hi,' I say. 'Can I come in?' Sally steps to one side, wordlessly, and I walk into the hallway.

'I was just washing the kitchen floor,' she says in a flat tone.

'Carry on,' I say.

'No, I'll leave it,' she says. She sighs and tugs off the rubber gloves. She opens the door into the sitting room and looks at me without smiling. This must be the first time I've seen her in, what? Three months? I can't help noticing how much she's aged, and how pinched her face is – all puckered around her eyes. I picture her as she used to look, back when I first knew her. Back when Mike still thought she was gorgeous. (Who knows, maybe he still does.) Sally was curvy and voluptuous then, with thick dark hair. She's grey now – streaked and flecky like a piece of granite. But then, so am I if I don't fake the colour.

'Do you want some coffee?' Sally says. She says it a bit reluctantly as if she'd prefer not to make the offer but is too polite not to. In the old days I'd have made my own while she scrubbed the kitchen floor. I'd have sat up on the kitchen bench with my legs dangling while she squeezed and swabbed and moaned about David . . . or the kids . . . or her mother. It's very odd to seem so much like strangers.

'Please,' I say. 'That would be nice.'

Sally makes coffee and brings it into the sitting room on a tray. It all feels very formal – as if I'm the health visitor calling, or the vicar, or some person she's never met before doing one of those surveys on a clipboard. Like a health visitor (or a vicar, or a person doing a survey) I ask a series of questions. They're safe questions, on the whole. Non-threatening. How's Becci's swimming? How's David? How's Sally's mum? Is Sally back at work yet? How is the woman next door who had triplets?

Sally gives brief unemotional answers. Becci's still swimming. David's fine. Sally's mum had her hip replacement and is doing OK. Sally *isn't* back at work. The woman next door shouts at her husband a lot and looks as if she never has a good night's sleep. I smile at this, remembering how we used to compare notes when our kids were small, when the broken nights were making us feel deranged. I wonder if Sally's thinking the same thing because I see the faintest flicker of a smile pass across her face too.

We drink our coffee and I eat a custard cream – more because I don't want to refuse than because I actually fancy it. It isn't the best or the easiest conversation we've ever had. It's awkward and the words don't flow. But at least we're in the same room . . . and talking.

Neither of us mentions Matt. We skirt round him, like pedestrians stepping round a great hole in the road.

By the time our question and answer session has dried up I've finished my drink. Sally is fiddling with her yellow gloves so I stand up and start to button my jacket. Now I'm walking towards the door, speaking empty pleasantries about how nice it's been to see her, how kind she was to make me delicious coffee, how well she is looking . . . but I feel I have to say *some*thing so I take the plunge and say, 'Matt wrote to me, Sally. I don't know if he told you?' She doesn't answer. She is fussing with the empty cups – putting them back on the tray, brushing biscuit crumbs off the arm of the sofa. I continue, 'I've written to him a couple of times now. I wanted him to know that . . . well, when he comes out, he's welcome . . . round at our house.' I wonder as I say this if it's strictly true. Will Mike feel the same way I do? Will Jack? Or Ben? Will I feel this magnanimous when I actually see him? I'm not sure. But I'm feeling hopeful. (Perhaps it's something to do with the new shoots in the garden this morning.)

'I'm hoping to go and visit him,' I say. 'Maybe before Christmas. If they'll let me – seeing as I'm not family . . .'

Sally looks up. Her eyes are moist. She is holding the tray in front of her, pressed against her chest like a shield. I reach out and take it from her and set it gently down on the coffee table. Sally stands with her arms by her sides, looking at the floor. Her hair has tumbled across her face but I can tell without seeing that she is crying. I step towards her and stretch out my arms, terrified that she will flinch away, or turn her back on me, or ask me to leave . . . But instead she hugs me, pressing her cheek into my shoulder. She hugs me so hard it makes my ribs ache. I hug her back and we both cry – like two orphans lost in a wood. Like Hansel and Gretel.

When we pull apart, I wipe my face and say, 'Will you come with me, when I go and see him?' and Sally nods.

Elliott

I've kept in touch with Matt while he's been inside. It's not been easy. I can't text him because he isn't allowed his phone – though texting Matt's a bit of a sore point anyway (I still feel like shit that it was *me* he was texting when it all happened). Matt says there are call boxes he can use – though they're not very private. I can't call *him*, but he can ring out. Apparently the better behaved he is, the more telephone minutes he gets. Yeah, really! He clocks up points, like those stars they used to give you in primary school. I remember even then – in Mrs Wyman's class – Matt used to have more stars on the chart than everyone else. (Teacher's pet!)

I do most of the talking when he calls – partly because Matt hasn't got much news, partly because he hates the way the guards listen in and smirk. I tell him daft stuff – funny stories, bits of goss. It's been harder since we all left school in the summer. Everyone's doing different things and there's a lot of the old crowd I hardly ever see. I see Ben though, and Pete. We've formed a new band. Rootstrings fell apart as soon as Matt wasn't there. We play the same old stuff but we're not as good. We could do with a good bass player . . .

Personally I think it's bloody ridiculous that they banged him up. As if the accident itself wasn't enough punishment. Matt was traumatised. Who wouldn't have been? Everyone thought the sentence was harsh. It felt like they were deliberately making an example of him – 'Don't drive and use your phone, kids! Let Matt Fry be a lesson to you all!' – and all that crap . . .

I was really rough the day after the party. Mum says I was sick fifteen times. (I'll take her word for it.) I slept for the whole day. Emma called me in the evening to tell me about the crash. She couldn't believe I didn't already know.

I walked along Broadfarm Road the next morning. I'm not sure why – it was a bit sick and ghoulish really. A bit like rubber-necking. Maybe I needed to see for myself because I couldn't quite believe it had happened. Like I needed proof or something.

There was proof all right. They'd taken the car away by then but there were gouges in the grass verge and bits of glass in the gutter. The mashed bus shelter completely freaked me out. I kept saying the F word over and over under my breath.

There were already mountains of flowers. Jesus!

On Broadfarm Road a man with tattooed arms is walking urgently towards a silver car. Suddenly – mercifully – he hears a wail of sirens, drowning out the sound of the screaming girl. Blue lights spin round the bend. Three vehicles – an ambulance and two police cars.

Inside the crumpled car, the driver sits upright, stiff with shock, the air bag deflated in his lap like a punctured beach ball. He is spotted with fine white dust, like chalk. The ambulance pulls up at the side of the road. A paramedic climbs out and walks towards the bloodstained girl she sees staggering along the grass verge. Tenderly, she steers the girl towards the ambulance tailgate and starts swabbing at the blood, staunching its flow. Two policemen are setting out an arc of cones in the road. Another walks towards the driver's side of the silver Corsa and opens the door. Now Matt is getting out, standing up, walking away from the car. Becci sees him through the fog of gauze and bandages. She sees that he is walking. Unharmed.

A fire engine screeches up, and three crew

members jump out. They have cutting equipment – axes and saws, like tree surgeons. They start to hack and slice, prising bent metal, scattering shards of glass. They need to extract a blonde-haired girl from the front passenger seat of the car. She is hard to reach – slumped forward, unconscious. But she is not dead. The paramedics find a pulse – the faintest of flickers. Matt can see her, trapped inside the wreckage of the car – now that he is outside, now that he is free. He wants to touch her but the paramedics won't let him through.

'Sophie,' he says. 'Oh God, Oh God, Oh God . . .'

There is so much blood. A woman police officer with a kind face takes his arm and leads him to a waiting police car.

The girl in a long white dress is lying down on a stretcher now. The blood on her cheek is starting to congeal. Men in green overalls have fitted a neck brace around her chin – just in case – and the woman who mopped her face is shining a light into her eyes. The girl is agitated. She wants to know where Nathan is and what's happening to Matt. She wants to know if Sophie will live. The paramedic strokes her forehead gently.

Now the girl in the bunny ears is being pulled from the wreckage. Her fishnet tights are slit to ribbons. A tartan dressing gown, soaked brown with blood, catches on a piece of jagged metal and is dragged from her, tearing. They put her on a stretcher, fasten on wires and tubes and bags. Her arms hang limply by her sides. Her face is waxy and motionless. Carefully – so carefully – they lift her into the ambulance, close the doors, and start the siren blaring again.

Just metres away, Matt is sitting in the back seat of one of the police cars. He sees the frantic blue light whirling past the window and feels sick with dread. Two traffic police are asking him questions, swabbing his fingers, making him breathe into a breathalyser, telling him to try and reconstruct the sequence of events. Matt feels numb. His mind is a chaos of images – details spinning as though an explosion has hurled them outwards into space, like so many disassembled fragments that will not stay still, will not come together. A fox, headlights, music, his hands clasping the wheel, screaming, darkness. He cannot remember. Cannot make sense of it all. He wants to see Becci. The police officer tells him she has gone to A and E.

Now the firemen are extricating the fourth passenger. They work less carefully this time, less urgently. This one is definitely dead. No need to lift him gently. They cut like butchers, hauling flesh from metal. On the pavement, on top of the crunching frost of broken glass, an unzipped body bag is lying ready.

Becci

Matt was hardly hurt at all because of the air bag. It puffed up like a huge blob of bubble gum, pressing against his face and chest, as if someone was attempting to smother him with a giant cushion, momentarily obscuring his view.

Sophie had been thrown against the door – or, more technically, the 'A' Pillar as the pathologist's report called it, which is the upright panel between the windscreen and the front door. Matt couldn't reach her and he couldn't see her either, which was just as well.

After the bang, Matt was silent for what seemed like an age. It was probably only a few seconds but it was long enough for me to think he was dead. I reached out my hand and felt the top of his head poking over the headrest of the seat in front. His hair was damp and sticky.

'Matt?' I said. Then again, getting louder and more desperate. 'Matt! MATT!' I'll never forgive him for not answering me straight away!

'MATT!' I said again, 'Are you alive?'

That was when he spoke.

'Becci?' was all he said.

Then I started speaking to Sophie and Nathan, calling out their names.

'Nathan? Sophie? NATH! SOPH!' There was no response.

With so little light it was hard to see. I could just make out Sophie's hair and the side of her face and a dark river running from her ear. But I couldn't get to her past the bulk of Nathan's legs.

The mess on the back seat was appalling. It was difficult to make out which was Nathan, which was the costume and which was the car upholstery. I groped about with my hands, feeling glass, metal, pieces of foam, nylon feathers . . . Everything was wet and there was a terrible smell. Warm splashes of blood were dripping onto my lap, onto my palms. Bit by bit I realised the blood was coming from me, from my face.

Then I felt Nathan's hand. It was unmistakably dead. I never knew dead bodies cooled so quickly. It was cold, heavy, gelatinous – like a piece of cod. I pulled my hand away, horrified.

That was when I lost it. I got out of the car, screaming. I should have dragged Matt out with me – the police said we were lucky the car didn't burst into flames . . . But I didn't.

I didn't try and help the others. I just wanted to escape. I just ran . . .

Matt

I've done nearly seven months now. They'll release me after Christmas – all being well – and I'll do the second half of my sentence in the community, under supervision – sleeping in my own bed again.

It's Saturday. I'm killing time, here in my cell, laid on my bed, waiting for my visit to start. The bed is narrow, with a hard mattress, low to the ground. Bleached sheets. Thin blanket. No duvet. Definitely a prison bed. No attempt at comfort. Sleeping in it is like a minute-by-minute reminder that you're being punished – made to feel bad, all night long.

Saturday's the only visiting time I get. One hour. Once a week. Mostly I look forward to it but sometimes I dread it. Seeing Dad, Mum, Becci makes me feel crap. 'Ashamed', more precisely. (Prison hasn't done much for my vocabulary.) Perhaps that's part of the 'Young Offender Institute' rationale – make the little buggers feel really guilty for what they've done to their poor families. Well, if that's the logic, then it works. After they've gone, I usually feel grim. Just seeing them, and hearing about all the things I'm missing, makes me ache to be home again.

Mum hasn't been for over a month but she wrote during the week to say she was coming today. I wonder how she'll look, how she'll be. She never looks at me any more. Not properly. Not eye-to-eye. I can't bear the way she's changed – what it's all done to her. And Becci, with her purple gash – like some badly stitched rip in a pair of jeans. She'll have to live with that for the rest of her life – and so will I. So will all of us . . .

I was pretty low when I first came in. So low they put me in Reo – the Reorientation wing (which is a polite name for segregation unit) – for a fortnight. You go into Reo because you're either bad or mad. Either you're a headcase and you've smashed up your cell or thrown a mug of hot water in someone's face or attacked a teacher with a pottery spatula, or you're a sad case – so 'vulnerable' they think you might try and top yourself. Either way they put you by yourself twenty-four hours a day and watch you all the time through a glass portal – all of which makes you feel worse than ever. I think they put me in Reo because I kept waking up screaming. And because they thought I might get bullied because I was clever – and soft.

I didn't actually want to top myself – not seriously – except maybe on the first night The first night is like being put out on a mountainside in the snow – like they used to put Spartan babies out to see if they were strong enough to survive. (Tough if they weren't, or if wolves came and ate them.)

They brought me here directly from the court. There was no time for fond farewells. No time to get used to the shock. Just a judge announcing my sentence and then – Bam! – into the Reliance van. Inside, those vans are full of individual padded cells, which is why they call them 'sweat boxes'. It stank to high heaven in there. The journey seemed endless and I was retching by the time they let me out.

They manhandled me in through the door – like I was going to do a jail break or something – and then they 'processed' me. Which goes like this: first they identify you, then they photograph you, then they fingerprint you, then they fill in half a million forms, then they take away everything you possess except your trainers and your boxer shorts. Things like watches, phones, beads, money go into your 'possessions bag'. (Apparently you get these back when you leave – unless they've been nicked and sold on the black market.) Having taken most of your clothes they make you strip naked. They search you, weigh you, give you a medical examination, and make you take a shower. (At least they don't shave your head, like in a Nazi concentration camp.) When you come out of the shower they give you a cosy bathrobe (nice touch that) but then as soon as you're dry, they take it off you and give you your prison uniform. It isn't striped pyjamas with arrows on them (unfortunately) – it's bottle green sweat shirts and track suit bottoms – like primary school without the cheery pump bag. Once you're all dressed and tidy they give you a meal and a hot cup of tea (not bread and water, then?) and then they present you with a menu sheet for the week and ask you to select your food. Food? As if they think you feel like food after all that.

I'm hungry now. I make myself a cup of orange squash and eat my last Rich Tea biscuit. I can buy biscuits and drinks (plastic bottles only – no cans, so we can't throw them at each other) in the shop, with my prison allowance – along with soap, toothpaste and deodorant (the roll-on type, not aerosols – in case we spray it in the guards' faces). You aren't allowed to buy more than two of anything so that people can't stock-pile stuff and then deal in it for tobacco.

They really have thought of everything.

I sit on my bed and dunk the biscuit in the watery orange. Dunking is a simple pleasure – a daily ritual. It's something I've always done but somehow I appreciate more in here where there's so little pleasure and so much time to fill. I dunk my Rich Tea slowly, almost reverently . . . A blob of it breaks off and sinks to the bottom of the cup.

I had post today – two items. A letter from Nathan's mum (Stella) and a postcard from Dan, one of my mates from the climbing club. Stella's started writing a lot – which is pretty nice of her. Today's letter's quite jokey and light. There's a funny story about Monty – the Jeffersons' dog – who's old and farts a lot. Stella writes about how he jumped into the lake at Sandwell park and a swan attacked him. I read it again . . . 'I've never seen him swim so fast getting out – he could hardly walk the next day!' I imagine Monty, with his floppy ears and his arthritic joints – imagine stroking his manky ginger fur, imagine playing with his velvety ears. That's how I spend hours and hours in here – imagining the things I miss. Trying to make them seem so real it's like I'm somewhere else and doing something else. That must be how people survive when they have nothing – like those blokes that were held hostage in Beirut – chained to radiators for years on end in total darkness. Or like that guy in *Touching the Void*, that climber who crawled back down the mountain even though he was almost dead. When people have got nothing left, they *make* things in their heads and that keeps them going.

Dan's postcard is a picture of Mont Blanc. The guys from the climbing club were planning a trip to Mont Blanc last summer. We'd been planning it for a whole year. I was one of the ones who most wanted to go. I look at the photograph Dan's sent me of the jagged snowy peak. It looks like they made it, then. But that was in August. How come the postcard's taken so long to arrive? I look at the postmark but it's too smudged to read. So then I start thinking: did it get lost in the post or did Dan spend four months worrying about whether he should send it to me or not? Worrying he might make me feel too bad? Or did the prison guards confiscate it and hide it – so I'd be deprived of the sight of mountains and snow? The sight of freedom . . .

I start to think about how much I miss mountains and fresh air and rain and mud but I sense myself starting to spiral downwards so I pick up Stella's letter and read about Monty again and picture the angry swan, hissing in his face.

They gave me counselling in the first couple of months. It was supposed to help with the nightmares, and the guilt. I can't tell if it worked or not. I have no way of knowing how I'd have been without it. Whether I'd have been better or worse. Anyway the therapy's finished now, but I still get visits from Paul – the chaplain. ('Rev Paul' people call him.) Paul's cool. He doesn't look like a vicar. No dog collar. He wears a purple polo shirt and an earring and he swears a lot. Paul's big on the Prodigal Son – which is a story I remembered from primary school. It's that story in the Bible about the cocky son who asked for his share of his dad's will before his dad had actually died and then went off and wasted all the money in a distant land. He's cheeky as well as cocky. Once he's skint, and starving and miserable, he decides to go back home again. You'd have thought his dad would tell him to piss off but he doesn't – he welcomes him back with open arms. Better than that, he actually runs out to meet the son when he sees him coming. Paul says that's the bit that would have been the most shocking in Jesus' day. The running. Apparently running in public was a complete no-no for a respectable man – it was a sign of great indignity. Something you just didn't do.

Coincidentally (or maybe not coincidentally, if Paul had anything to do with it) the chapel here is called 'The Prodigal Son Chapel'. There's a painting on the wall outside of a skinny bloke being hugged by a man with a beard like Father Christmas. It's a bit naff. The Father Christmas figure looks a bit dodgy and the skinny bloke's head is too small in proportion to the rest of his body. But it's better than I could do. Paul says one of the trainees did it. (Notice that, they call us 'trainees' instead of 'inmates'. It's more positive. It emphasises rehabilitation rather than punishment. It's all part of the friendly regime – like the casual polo shirts, and the floral curtains, and calling the staff by their first names. Still iron bars on the windows though.)

There's a famous painting of the Prodigal Son by the artist Rembrandt. I remember looking at it in art at school – doing a rubbish copy of it in oil pastels. I told Paul this one day and he brought me a little postcard print of the same painting. I keep it by my bed. It's a fantastic picture. The son is kneeling in front of his father – with his back to the camera, as it were. He's got bare feet and a shaved head and he's holding onto the older man, round the waist – burying his face into his father's clothes. The thing I like best is the father's hands. Their whiteness stands out against the darker colours. The hands are resting on the son's back, spread calmly across his shoulder-blades – gently holding him. Sometimes, at night, I just lie and look at it.

Nighttimes are the worst. They lock us in our cells at eight o'clock and then the time just drags on interminably till morning. I hate the clanking of the doors at bang-up time – the way the metallic slam and the grinding of the keys echoes all round the wing. And I hate the way thoughts ambush me in the darkness – screams, screeching tyres, Nathan's voice yelling at me – 'Put the fucking brakes on!'

But I can't complain. After all, I'm alive and Nathan isn't. And it hasn't all been bad. I've worked hard. No distractions. Seriously focussed. I did my A levels as planned. Sat the papers all by myself in the education block. I couldn't do Business Studies because finishing the coursework was too complicated but I did History and Politics, the same as I would have done, and I picked up English and sat an A level in that. I did pretty well considering it was early days here and I was still feeling like a fish out of water. I reckon reading and studying kept me sane in the first couple of months. Now I work in the kitchens five days a week. I've even passed my food hygiene certificate! And the exercise – that's another good thing. There's a great gym where we have to go three times a week – no arguments, no choice. I'm probably fitter than I was when I came in and I've got pretty good at basketball too – which will amaze my mates, since at school I was always rubbish. There's even a climbing wall in the gym. It's a pretty basic one – beginner standard really – but it's given me something to do. I've actually done a bit of coaching recently – helping the younger lads get their confidence with the ropes.

They keep us busy as much as possible so we're less likely to cause trouble. In the evenings – before lock-up – we have to do 'Association' which is clubs and stuff. There's a music club on a Monday night where I get to play guitar – though not mine obviously. (I even play bass in the chapel services, which, surprisingly, I really like.) Mostly, in association, I play table football or pool. I'm shit hot at pool these days.

Plus I've learnt a whole new language. I call cigarettes 'burn'. I know that 'taxing' means black-market trading and that being 'spun' means having your cell searched. I know that 'hooch' is illegal alchohol made by soaking chunks of bread in orange juice and hiding them somewhere in your cell in an old sock. This stuff will really come in useful on the outside!

But the best thing is it's nearly over. My sentence will be finished in the spring. Cardiff deferred my place so I can go to uni in September if I want to – I got the grades I needed. So it's been a sort of 'gap year' – a gap year with a difference, if that doesn't sound too flippant. I'm going to go and climb Mont Blanc in August if I can save up enough money in time. One thing is certain. I won't be coming back here.

There's a guy called Wez on our wing who's been in and out thirteen times since he was twelve. Every time he gets released he goes and reoffends within days. He's a nice enough lad – he just can't stop nicking things. Then there's Zak in the cell next to mine who came in the week after me. He's seventeen and he's doing five years for rape. Zak's got a kid – a baby boy called Abraham with chubby cheeks. By the time Zak gets out Abraham will be at school. Zak's girlfriend comes to visit him and brings the baby too. She's quite pretty – skinny and blonde with hair a bit like Sophie's.

I can't cope with thinking about Sophie. When I

first came in I had a photo of her on my cell wall but I took it down because it made me feel too dire. Paul says I should write to her mum and dad. He says I need to ask for their forgiveness. Yeah sure, Paul.

'How can I expect them to forgive me when I can't forgive myself?' I said one day, when he was paying me a pastoral visit. Paul got really angry and threw a book at me across the cell. He said I was wallowing in self-pity.

'If God can forgive you, why can't you forgive yourself?' he shouted. 'Do you think you're better than God?' I didn't really have an answer to that one.

I look in the mirror above my sink and comb my hair. It must be nearly time. I get a quick spasm of nervousness in my stomach, worry that I won't be able to think of anything to say.

Then I hear my name. 'Matthew Fry. Time.'

I hear the key turn in the lock, see the door swing open, step out into the lobby and walk down the draughty corridor in front of the guard.

Becci

Matt was never a particularly trendy dresser but he had a certain sense of style. He had cool hair – thick and dark and slightly wavy – which he wore quite long and layered and he'd put wax in it to make it look bed-headish. He wore nice jewellery too – leather stuff and chunky metal beads. He had a stone cross on a leather shoe lace that I really liked and a great studded belt. He was always quite careful about what he wore and positively fussy about the clothes he'd choose if he was going for a night out – especially after he started going out with Sophie – and he'd do subtle things like colour-co-ordinating his socks. I remember once Sophie said she really liked that. I hadn't really noticed he did it before she said so. She said it showed he was 'sensitive'.

Matt's hair is much shorter now – no gel or hair putty. (Against regulations apparently.) And he looks nerdy in the dark green sweat shirt – a bit like a boy scout who's lost all his badges and his neck-scarf-thingy.

I watch Matt come into the visitor room flanked by two guards in black puffa jackets. One guard is big and beefy. The other has a smiley face and looks a bit like that guy off the Halifax ad. They've both got those black head-set microphones like aerobics instructors. Halifax man escorts Matt over to where we're sitting. Dad stands up and steps out awkwardly from behind the bolted-down table. 'Hi,' he says and he opens his arms and gives Matt a long hug. I hug Matt too, which is something I didn't use to do before. We were never a very huggy family but since Matt's been inside we've all started doing these 'big-hug' love-ins, like the Teletubbies.

Matt feels skinny and he's looking spotty now I see him up close. He's very pale too. *Before*, he always used to have rosy cheeks – very rugged and healthy looking. Now he smells wrong too – smoky and sort of institutional, as if he's been disinfected.

'You nicked my poodle jumper,' he says, tugging at my sleeve.

'Do you mind?' I say. He grins, so I assume that means he doesn't.

We sit down on the plastic chairs.

'Mine's a cheese burger with extra fries,' Dad says. He always makes this joke. Something about the furniture, he says.

'I wish,' says Matt wistfully.

'Do you want a coffee?' Dad says. There's a vending machine by the window. I watch an obese silver-haired woman – someone's grannie maybe? –

getting a cup of hot chocolate and slopping it down her coat.

'No thanks,' Matt says. He looks preoccupied. 'Where's Mum?' he asks and I get a sinking feeling as Dad starts to make excuses for her.

'She wasn't feeling too well . . . had a bit of a bad night . . . would have loved to be here . . . sent her love . . .' Blah blah blah. I wish she'd just *come* so Dad doesn't have to go through this every time. Matt nods. I can't tell if he's disappointed or relieved.

'So what's been happening?' Dad says, attempting to change the subject. He sounds absurdly cheery – as if he's trying too hard – but Matt plays the game, dutifully. He gives us a round-up of the highlights of his week, such as they are – tells us a few funny stories about life in the kitchens, recounts how Wez's cell got spun and they found hooch under his bed. Tells us about a nasty incident with a plastic fork after which three trainees ended up in Reo.

Then he says, casually, 'Oh, and they made me a Platinum Boy.'

'Platinum?' I squeal. 'Wow! I thought Gold was the highest level you could get.'

'It's new,' Matt says, 'there are only three of us.'

'That's great, Matt,' Dad says, beaming at him. Dad likes achievements – even if it's just accumulating Nectar points in prison.

They have this reward scheme where you get

privileges in exchange for good behaviour. The more co-operative you are, the nicer they make your life. That way, there's more to lose when you screw up, and so – the theory goes – you're less likely to cause trouble and risk jeopardising your 'regime'.

Everybody starts on Bronze level and then you can progress up to Silver, Gold, and now Platinum (what next?) – provided you play the game. 'Bronze Boys' have the worst time of all. (Apparently there are always lots of Bronze Boys in chapel because, by pretending to be religious, you can wangle more time out of your cell.) Matt went onto the Gold regime in October. That meant less time locked up, more table football, longer showers and access to the hot-water machine so he could make himself cups of tea. It also meant he got to use the climbing wall in the gym, which he was pretty pleased about.

'So what does Platinum mean?' I ask. 'That you get to sleep in a four-poster bed?'

Matt grins. 'It means I can have the Playstation in my cell after bang-up. And . . . I can make toast in the kitchen in Association time.'

'Cool!' I say. Then I remember the food I've brought him so I hand over the Waitrose carrier bag.

'It's been searched,' I say. 'So there are no ecstasy tablets in the Crunchie.'

'Shame,' says Matt. He rummages in the bag, pulls out a satsuma, peels one and gives us both a piece.

'Have you had any news about your release date?'
Dad says.

Matt nods, biting the end off a segment of orange
and sucking out the juice. 'Nothing definite,' he says.
'Hugh came on Wednesday. He's says it's looking
good for the New Year.'

'That's great, Matt,' Dad says. 'I'll give him a call.'

Hugh's our solicitor – Matt's solicitor. He's a friend
of Dad's – his squash partner in fact – and he's a really
nice bloke. During the trial he was very supportive.
Afterwards he was shocked at the harshness of
Matt's sentence – he said he didn't think Matt would
get custodial in the light of all his squeaky-clean
character references. I suppose if you've killed two
people it doesn't make much difference whether
you've helped old ladies across the street and been
kind to kittens. There are still two dead people and
it's still your fault . . .

I hate the thought of Matt being inside for Christmas.
Imagine spending Christmas Day in prison. It makes
me think of that *Simpsons* episode when Bart thinks
he might get sent to jail for shop-lifting from Try-
and-Save and he day-dreams about a tawdry Father
Christmas coming to Juvenile Hall and giving all the
young offenders crumby presents like 'A book of
carpet samples' and 'A soiled wig'. Mum says we
can do Christmas late this year – have it in January

sometime when Matt gets home. She's hardly done anything towards Christmas yet. I know there's still a month to go but it's not like Mum. She's normally one of those smug people who get all their presents wrapped up and hidden away in the middle of October.

As if reading my thoughts Matt says, 'Is Mum all ready for Christmas then? Is the padlock on the bedroom cupboard?'

I say something vague and non-committal like 'What? Yeah!' and change the subject. I'm as bad as Dad, wanting to hide from Matt how much Mum's not coping.

I spot Zak's girlfriend Carla with their baby Abraham (cute name), across on the other side of the hall. Abraham's squirming around with stiff arms, looking hot and bad-tempered, and Zak's shaking a rattle in the baby's face, trying to stop him grizzling. Suddenly the baby stops kicking his legs, looks at Zak and smiles a huge sunny smile.

'Bless!' I say, watching them. Zak's really gorgeous – he looks like Thierry Henry. But I was spooked when Matt told me what he was serving time for. You just can't tell from looking at people. There's a kid on Matt's wing called Sean who looks like the sort of chubby kid who'd get teased a bit at school. Maybe he'd be a bit on the fringe of things. Matt says he killed some bloke with a hammer – bludgeoned him to death in cold blood. You'd never guess from looking at him. He looks so ordinary.

Dad's asking Matt if he's all right for money. He always asks that. What does Matt have to spend it on? Robinsons Barley Water and bars of soap!

'I had a letter from Stella,' Matt says, a bit out of the blue. I wonder if he's been looking for the right moment to say it. Stella's face comes into my mind. Her denim jacket. Her purple velvet scarf.

'She wants to come and see me . . .'

Matt is looking at the table, twiddling the cuff of his sweat shirt sleeve.

'That's very generous of her,' Dad says. We sit for a moment in silence. I'm thinking of Nathan – remembering the taste of him.

Then the guard comes over to our table.

'That's all for now, folks,' he says. 'Time's up.'

'Right . . .' Dad says, slapping his thighs, sounding decisive. He stands up. We hug each other again – enact the familiar ritual.

'Thanks for coming,'

'Have a good week.'

'Take care.'

'Give my love to Mum.' Same script every week.

This time Dad claps Matt on the forearm, stares

into his eyes and says, 'Well done, Matt – about the Platinum thing . . .' Matt shrugs.

I watch his back as they lead him away. As he reaches the doorway he glances back and gives us a muted smile. I wave, feeling suddenly choked up. I always hate this bit – always feel terribly sad. I remind myself that I'm going to see him again next Saturday. Imagine what it would be like if your brother was on death row and you had to say goodbye to him for the very last time. Like in *Green Mile*. (I watched that recently at Emma's house on DVD but I had to switch it off before the end. I can't stand prison movies any more.)

We go through sliding doors, along echoing corridors, past the sniffer dog, out into the lobby again. I hand in my tag and get my phone back. As we walk out into the car park I switch it back on. Two missed calls and a text – all from Emma.

'Do u wnt 2 cme rnd 2nite? Em'

I text back, 'Yes. Thanx.'

Sally

After Stella left I went upstairs. I went into Matt's bedroom, took off my shoes, folded back the covers and got into his bed. Even though the sheets are clean, even though no one's slept there for months, the bed still smells of Matt. I pulled the duvet up over my ears, sank down into the mattress, burrowed my face in the pillow.

I must have been there an hour or more.

I started thinking about the day Matt was born. About the hot-air balloon that went past the hospital window, the shafts of sunlight that spilled across his cheek as he slept beside me. No one tells you when you have a baby that being a mother will make you cry. That every time your child is hurting, you'll hurt too. That even when he's big and grown – old enough to have children of his own, old enough to live alone, old enough to drive a car – you'll still worry about him, fret about him, feel as if some invisible cord is coiled around your insides – tangled round the very core of you – connecting you to him.

Matt looked so desolate when David brought him home. He'd been arrested, David told me later.

Charged with Causing Death by Dangerous Driving. They'd released him on bail 'pending further enquiries'. I heard the key in the front door and came to, thinking it was Matt and Becci coming back from the party. When I rolled across and reached for David and found the bed was empty something made me get up, put on my dressing gown, and go to the top of the stairs. Some sixth sense intuition told me that something was wrong.

Matt was red-eyed from crying and his jeans were splattered with blood – God knows whose. I felt my legs turn weightless and my stomach lurch.

'Where's Becci?' I yelled.

From Matt's bed I could see the tree outside his window. Its bare branches had been covered in snow all day but now, in the late afternoon sun, they were dripping meltwater – like fat teardrops. I watched the drips sparkle as they caught the light.

Then I got up out of the bed and walked to the bathroom. That's where I am now. Amber rays from the low, wintry sun are slanting in at the window. I look in the mirror and see myself illuminated – artificially golden as if in some glowing holiday snap from a forgotten time – a distant land. Instinctively, unthinking, I smile at myself in the glass. Then – inspired – I reach for my make-up purse, tucked behind the curtain on the window sill, and take out a lipstick. I pull off the lid, twist the finger of pink out from its shellcase, look at its lustrous sheen. I brush the lipstick across my top lip, trace the line of the bow, sweep it across my bottom lip, pout, press both lips together. Smile again.

Matt

Sophie's dad rang me up the day before the hearing and said he hoped I'd get life. Actually he was even more over-the-top than that. He said, 'I hope you rot in hell.' I have these dread-filled daydreams of running into him once I'm out – in town maybe, outside Dixons or in JJB Sports – where he comes over and lays me out with his fists. Punches the living daylights out of me. (I never was much of a fighter.) I caught his eye as they led me out of court. His face was boiling with rage – so much hatred he looked like a volcano ready to blow. Sophie said he always had a temper. She said her mum used to lock herself in the bathroom when he was drunk.

He's not the only person I dread running into on the outside. There's Sophie's mum too, and her dad's new wife (the one with the baby and the leopard-skin shoes) and Nathan's brothers Ben and Jack. And Nathan's dad, Mike. And the bloke in the white van who's been off work for a year with a bad back – who sued us for compensation. Perhaps that's what prison is *really* for – to protect perpetrators of crime from all the people out there who hate their guts. At least in here I feel safe.

I walk from the visiting room, past the education block and out into the yard. It's 'Mass move' now and everyone's heading back from visits, so the route is lined with guards, bristling with radios and head sets, watching us like birds of prey. I skirt past the astro-turf five-a-side pitch, feeling the cold wind on my face, pausing momentarily to look up at the sky – to notice grey clouds swirling away from the sun – before someone steps towards me to hurry me on my way. Not even Platinum Boys get to loiter. I go through the sliding door into the residential wing, walk up the metal stairway to the first floor, make my way along the corridor to my cell door. They've painted our doors in vibrant colours to make the place look more cheerful. Less bleak. Mine is lilac – the same colour as Becci's bathrobe. But it's still a cell door. Metal. Impenetrable. With a spy flap that snaps open and shut – on the outside only. Beyond your control.

I step inside and the lilac door clangs shut. I hear the key crunch in the lock. Feel myself caged again.

I sit down on the floor with my back to the bed, knees crooked up, and take the Crunchie from the crinkly bag Becci gave me. Slowly, I tear off the wrapper and, unveiling the fat finger of chocolate, I press my nose against it, savour its smell. Then I bite it – just a tiny bite (I want to make it last) – just enough to expose the golden honeycomb centre. The chocolate is brittle. A fragment of it falls onto my knees and I pick it up, not wanting any of it to waste. Now I put my tongue against the sugary lava, feel the fizzy sensation of the cinder toffee, suck its sweetness.

I shut my eyes and think of home. Think of Becci, swamped by my grey sweater. Think of Dad's arms encircling me. Think of Mum laughing. Then I think of Mont Blanc. Bright sunlight. Dazzling snow. Pure mountain air. As the chocolate dissolves in my mouth, I imagine myself there – roped and secure, feeling for a foothold, clasping cold rock, slicing through the packed snow with my ice axe. Climbing. And free.

A note from the author

Damage was a difficult book
to write – writing it while my eldest son
was learning to drive didn't help. Describing
what Becci and Stella and Elliott go through, I asked
myself, 'How would that feel if it was my brother...
my son... my friend?' I became very aware of roadside
bouquets – traffic accidents seemed to be everywhere.
(Sadly, there have been two amongst my
children's peer group since I finished the book.)
Damage isn't a happy read, but if just one teenager
drives more carefully, or one parent cherishes their
child more tenderly as a result of reading it,
I will be thankful.